Fortuna

Fortuna

a novel

Fortuna
Nicholas Maes

ROCKY MOUNTAIN
BOOK AWARD
Alberta Children's Choice Book Award

DUNDURN
TORONTO

Editor: Shannon Whibbs
Design: Courtney Horner
Printer: Webcom

Library and Archives Canada Cataloguing in Publication

Maes, Nicholas, 1960-
        Fortuna / by Nicholas Maes.

(A Felix Taylor adventure)
Issued also in electronic formats.
ISBN 978-1-4597-0561-6

        I. Title. II. Series: Maes, Nicholas, 1960- . Felix
Taylor adventure.

PS8626.A37F67 2013   jC813'.6   C2012-907672-4

1   2   3   4   5   17   16   15   14   13

Conseil des Arts du Canada   Canada Council for the Arts   ONTARIO ARTS COUNCIL   CONSEIL DES ARTS DE L'ONTARIO

We acknowledge the support of the **Canada Council for the Arts** and the **Ontario Arts Council** for our publishing program. We also acknowledge the financial support of the **Government of Canada** through the **Canada Book Fund** and **Livres Canada Books**, and the **Government of Ontario** through the **Ontario Book Publishing Tax Credit** and the **Ontario Media Development Corporation**.

Care has been taken to trace the ownership of copyright material used in this book. The author and the publisher welcome any information enabling them to rectify any references or credits in subsequent editions.

J. Kirk Howard, President

Printed and bound in Canada.

VISIT US AT
Dundurn.com | @dundurnpress | Facebook.com/dundurnpress | Pinterest.com/dundurnpress

Dundurn
3 Church Street, Suite 500
Toronto, Ontario, Canada
M5E 1M2

Gazelle Book Services Limited
White Cross Mills
High Town, Lancaster, England
LA1 4XS

Dundurn
2250 Military Road
Tonawanda, NY
U.S.A. 14150

To my beloved family
I would gladly travel across time for you

Chapter One

*C*aesar brought his charger to a stop. The pair was standing in the middle of the river. As the current eddied about the horse's fetlocks, the general studied the terrain beyond. It was mostly open farmland and easily travelled. Enemy forces could be seen from a distance and its farms would be rich in provisions. All in all, this land was perfect ... apart from the fact that it was strictly off-limits.

The air was still. If Caesar closed his eyes, it would be easy to imagine he was alone in that landscape, so quiet were the soldiers of the thirteenth legion, even though they were marshalled directly behind him. There was no talk, no coughing, no groans of fatigue, never mind he'd pushed them mercilessly. They were gazing at the river, excited and abashed at their appointed task.

The river. It was maximum three ulnae *in breadth, a cubit deep, and its current was tame. It was nothing like the foreign rivers: the Arar, Rhodanus, Rhenus, Sequana, and, strangest of all, the winding Tamesis, its banks lined with Celts when he'd last sailed its waters. Such rivers could have swallowed his legion, unlike this Rubicon, which was just a feeble stream. And yet. On its northern bank he was a general of Rome; on its south he was nothing....*

"So? What's it to be?" a voice addressed him. Caesar smiled. His right-hand man Marcus Antonius had joined him.

"Ave Marce. It's a funny thing. On this bank I'm in Cisalpine Gaul. I'm its leader and can act as I please. Across this trickle lies Italy. On its soil my imperium *dies. If I lead my troops across, I'll no longer be Rome's champion but her back-stabbing son."*

"Don't tell me Caesar is getting cold feet? The victor of the Belgae, Suebi, and Helvetii has met a boundary that gives him pause?"

"You know how matters stand. If I cross my army over, I'll start a civil war. The Senate will pronounce me a hostis *— me, Julius Caesar, a loyal Roman! There will be no peace until I've crushed their troops, or they've crushed mine. Blood will be shed, good Roman blood, and the land will teem with widows and orphans."*

"So you won't cross? These troops have marched behind you in vain? The legions that did your bidding in Gaul and wish to see you honoured — you would spurn their dedication? You would have them disband and go home to their families?"

"The decision is too great for one man alone, even such a man as I."

Caesar considered the river. A mist was rising from its surface. The land on its far side was calling to him. The sun, too, was glaring down, either admiring Caesar's brashness or appalled by it. Retreat or attack, which would he choose? The issue lay beyond all human judgment and he needed ... help. He reached for the pouch that dangled from his cingulum.

"Are you consulting your mistress?" Antonius joked.

"She's never failed me yet," Caesar said. He was holding four astragali or knucklebones. Shaking them in his right hand, he muttered a prayer and rolled them onto his palm. With one brisk motion, he rolled them onto his open palm. He studied the effects and smiled grimly.

"What did you throw?" Antonius asked. His bantering was gone and he was serious now. Caesar held the bones out. "Mehercule! You've thrown a Venus!" Antonius cried. "Surely Fortuna must favour this venture."

"So it would seem," Caesar agreed, prodding his horse forward. "Signal the men. We'll cross the river and gamble on war. The knucklebones have spoken. Alea jacta est!"

A whistle startled Felix from his reading. His book, Suetonius's *Lives of the Caesars*, slipped from his fingers to the floor of his g-pod. He sat up straight and looked around. The passengers in the shuttle were sitting calmly and gave no sign of having heard the signal. He consulted a Teledata screen to see where they were. The craft was over Iceland and fifteen minutes from the depot in Toronto. So why the whistle?

"Honoured passengers," a voice broke in, "InterCity Services is pleased to inform you that Global President Siegfried Angstrom will be addressing the world in precisely five minutes. Please stay tuned for this important broadcast."

"I was expecting this," Stephen Gowan yawned. He was seated beside Felix and had engaged the speaker. How typical. Whenever he was on the same transport as Felix, he'd sit beside him and jabber away.

"What were you expecting?" Felix asked, retrieving his book.

"It's been a year," Stephen drawled, "since that problem started. I can't remember what the problem was, but the president must be speaking to mark the occasion."

Felix smiled ruefully. It was hard to believe that a year ago today a deadly plague had stormed the planet. Even harder to believe was his discovery of a text that had shown this plague had struck in Roman times and its cure back then had been the *lupus ridens*. Because the flower was extinct in 2213, he'd travelled back to ancient Rome, using the secret Time Projection Module (or TPM). Carolyn Manes had gone with him and together they'd tracked down the *lupus ridens*, brought it to the future, and stopped the plague in its tracks.

As incredible as this "mission" seemed, it was even crazier that people had forgotten the disaster. Once rescued from the jaws of destruction, the victims had shrugged and resumed their routines, as if their lives had never hung in the balance. Over the last twelve months, since the plague had been contained, not once had anyone referred to it in public, as if it had been a hiccup and nothing more. How could people forget so quickly?

How? That was obvious. Enhanced ERR. And Mem-rase.

"Honoured passengers," the voice spoke again, "InterCity Services is pleased to inform you that our Global President Siegfried Angstrom will be addressing the world in precisely three minutes. Please stay tuned for this important broadcast."

"Yeah right," Stephen smirked. "It will be as important as that book you're reading. What're you wasting your time on now?"

"Suetonius' *Lives of the Caesars*."

"As in Caesar salad?" Stephen joked.

"Caesar as in Julius. I found the book in Holland. It was left out in the garbage."

"That's where it belongs!" Stephen sneered. "You really are something. You could study genetics, programming, or syn-chem; instead you read these fairy tales! If you're not careful, you'll end up being useless."

As if to underline this point, the lights in the cabin flickered for an instant. This had happened a lot in recent days, and people just ignored it.

For his part, Felix shrugged. Whenever Stephen talked to him, the guy would go nuts about his interest in Latin. Felix always wanted to say it was his knowledge of Latin that had saved the world, not Stephen's precious computer skills. But like most folks, Stephen didn't remember the crisis and Felix couldn't disclose his exploits. When General Manes had shown him the TPM, Felix had been forced to swear that he wouldn't breathe a word about it, on pain of life imprisonment off-world. And when he'd flown to it in recent days, to spend time with Carolyn, the general had reminded him to keep his mouth shut.

But it was odd. For all the good his Latin had done, he was inclined to agree with Stephen Gowan.

Over the last six months his dad's health had been off. His condition wasn't serious, but he couldn't manage the Repository on his own — as Felix had often explained to Stephen, the Repository was the last collection of books on earth. This meant Felix had to help his dad out. Instead of studying math or syn-chem, as Stephen suggested, he spent his days roaming the planet and amassing books that needed saving. And when he wasn't hopping all over the place, he was cataloguing items and making repairs. The work was tedious, but necessary; otherwise the authorities would shut them down. And if the Repository closed, its books would perish.

But he often wondered: was this his future? He would rescue books and keep them safe for people who had no interest in them? He would master languages that were no longer spoken and study subjects that had long been forgotten? The Repository was a graveyard of ideas. Was this where he wanted to pass his days…?

"I spoke to Carolyn," Stephen said. "She said you're meeting later."

"Yeah. We're playing Halo Ball."

"Tell her to dress nicely tonight. And that my parents hate it when guests show up late."

"She's meeting your parents?"

"All of us are attending the awards ceremony."

"What awards ceremony?"

"Geez, you're out of it, aren't you? I won a contest. Carolyn came in second. Boy, she hated losing."

Again the lights wavered briefly.

Felix was too distracted to question this flickering. Six months ago he and Carolyn had been flying to Prague to rescue yet another cache of books. They'd been debating the novel ERR limits when Stephen had told them to keep it down. Felix had introduced Carolyn to Stephen and she'd taken a shine to the geek. Since then, the pair had seen a lot of one another….

"Honoured passengers," a voice broke in, "InterCity Services is pleased to inform you that our Global President Siegfried Angstrom will be addressing the world in precisely ten seconds. Please stay tuned for this important broadcast."

"And she should adjust her skin tone," Stephen added. "She's way too pale."

Before Felix could answer, a face appeared on every screen in the transport: Siegfried Angstrom.

As always he looked terrific, with his leonine nose, stark blond hair, and glacier-blue eyes — his retinal implants augmented their brightness. Felix was thrown back a year, to the night he'd called the Angstrom Show and revealed that the *lupus ridens* might be a cure for the plague. Angstrom had ignored him with withering contempt.

He was even more forbidding now. Felix thought of Sajit Gupta, the former president. Unlike Angstrom, who was ice in human form, Gupta had been warm and friendly. That's why Angstrom had thrust him aside.

Once the world recovered from the plague, it had reviewed Gupta's stewardship and found it wanting. People thought that he'd shown too much feeling; there was a rumour, too, that he'd had his Emotional Range Reduction (ERR) removed. Disgusted with his feely-mealy ways, the population had forced him to resign. Elections had followed and Angstrom had won.

Because he'd run on an anti-feeling platform, his first act was to broaden the ERR range. The effects were obvious. When Felix talked with strangers, he might have been addressing a pile of rocks. It had been months since he'd heard anyone weep, scream, or laugh. And because he refused to endure the treatment himself, people thought that *he* was the freak when he smiled, frowned, or spoke with feeling.

While ERR was bad, Mem-rase was worse. This too was Angstrom's doing. Convinced the past had nothing to teach them, he'd broadened the old

Mem-rase program, permitting citizens to delete their memories of the plague. This was why people couldn't recall the disaster.

And there was more. Because Angstrom had no attachment to the past, his officials found the Repository to be a waste of funds. Over the last few months, e-briefs had arrived, to the effect that the Repository was being "reconsidered," a fancy way of saying it would be closed in future. In fact …

"Greetings," Angstrom spoke, interrupting his thoughts, "let me get straight to the point. It has been one year since we faced that 'disruption' and, after hesitating greatly, I decided to mark the occasion. Why my hesitation, you'll ask? Because by mentioning the 'disruption,' I might seem to be admitting that we erred somehow, that luck saved us more than anything else, and that we must change the way we confront the world, from our science-bound perspective to something more emotional. But this is not my intention at all."

Angstrom bristled here, as if daring viewers to challenge this statement. Felix thought the former talk host was glaring straight at him.

"Let me emphasize right now that we did everything right. It was our cold, hard reasoning that saw us through, and if we owe a debt to anyone, it's to our engineers and scientists. Luck didn't achieve our success, just as our 'feelings' had nothing to do with it, either. In fact, if we erred in any way, it was by relying too much on 'feelings' and 'luck,' as if these had more to deliver than science and logic. If the 'disruption' taught us anything, it's that we need more science and less of everything else."

"Did you hear that?" Stephen barked. "Science saves us, not your stupid books."

"Shortly after the disruption," Angstrom continued, "I was voted in as president and decided that, yes, some changes would be productive. But far from rejecting our reasoned outlook, I was determined to embrace it even more than before. That's why my first act was to broaden ERR and to place an even greater brake on our emotions. I also urged citizens to enroll in the new Mem-rase program and thereby reduce our ties to the past. Have my initiatives borne fruit? I'll leave that to the people to decide, but it is worth pointing out global efficiency rates have never been higher."

When he said the word "efficiency," the lights wavered off and on.

"He's so cool," Stephen crooned, oblivious to the lights. "One day I hope to be like him."

"I wish to leave you with two thoughts," Angstrom concluded. "First, the hallmark of our lives is utility, not humour, art, beauty, or sentiment. We humans are at our best when we're useful, not effusive. More to the point, we belong to the future. There's no utility in looking to the past, only embarrassment that, for so long, we depended on luck and emotion to save us. That's why I urge you, having honoured the scientists who steered us to safety, to jettison this 'disruption' to the junk heap that is history. The past is over. Let's delete it from our hard drives. By focusing on the future alone, we'll ensure good order and logic prevail."

Angstrom glared at them one final time and his face quickly melted. It was replaced by a map showing the shuttle's position. They were flying over Labrador.

"What a guy," Stephen crowed. "I'm glad I had my memories erased, the ones involving that stupid 'disruption.'"

Felix was distressed by the speech. Aware he couldn't speak his mind, he was about to make some lukewarm comment when a full-blown power outage cut him short. One moment every system was working; the next every screen fell blank, the lights died completely and the engine was silent. Their steady flight slowed and … the craft started falling.

Within seconds they'd built up a terrific speed. The craft was nosing downward and Felix's knees were at his ears. There was a crushing sensation on his chest and face. His head was pounding. He was dripping sweat. He'd never been so scared before; at the back of his throat a scream started forming.

As abruptly as it had failed, the power returned. The engine was humming, the lights flicked on, and the craft swiftly straightened itself. Every screen was back online and a voice was explaining that the ship was fine and InterCity Services regretted the outage.

Felix tried to calm himself. He took deep breaths and pressed his hands together, even as he looked the cabin over. His heart almost stopped. Everyone was calm. They'd been faced with death mere seconds before, yet they were serene, bored, utterly unfazed. As if nothing untoward had happened, Stephen was saying that Carolyn should dress in blue that evening.

The fear Felix had experienced when the craft had failed? It was nothing like his terror just then, faced as he was with a crowd of human robots.

Chapter Two

*T*he August sun was burning hot and threatening to scour the plain of Pharsalus. The Enipeus River was almost boiling over, while the trees were shrinking into themselves. Already birds were wheeling on high. They weren't bold enough to descend just yet, not with troops strolling among the corpses, but knew they would feed when evening arrived. They numbered less than fifty then. Within minutes their flocks would be so thick that they would shade the plain against the dazzling sun.

Caesar was picking his way through the carnage. Four hours back, his position had been bleak: Pompey's troops had outnumbered his, had better provisions and occupied the high ground. For someone who'd beaten impossible odds, Caesar didn't look pleased. His expression was pained more than anything else. His left fist, too, was tightly clenched.

The scene was awful. Corpses littered the soil as far as the eye could see. In some places they were lined up, as if Death had reaped them with one blow of his scythe. In others they were heaped in piles, some as high as a two-storey house. Many of the bodies exhibited multiple wounds. One centurion had three pila *in his chest and an arrow in his thigh. His hand was gripping on to his sword whose blade was buried in his killer's neck — for all eternity they'd embrace each other so. There were headless corpses, legless corpses, armless corpses and unblemished ones. Perhaps their hearts had suddenly stopped or terror had kept their lungs from drawing breath.*

And then there were the horses. There was nothing so graceful as a horse in full canter and nothing so awkward as one in death. Their legs seemed to multiply when death stilled their movements; they burst from a trunk at impossible angles and seemed to kick fretfully in every direction, as if unable to believe their lives had been stilled.

And the blood. There was a sea of it. A man who has seen the aftermath of battle understands that living things are leathern sacks of red dye. Intelligence, wit, athletic skill, and kindness are reduced in final analysis to this, a lake of blood that even Charon couldn't chart with his raft.

It was comic how people would distinguish blood: a senator's or patrician's was richer than a pleb's. Was there anyone on that field of battle who could tell the blood of optimi *from the gore of common soldiers?*

"Ave Caesar!" a voice called out. "Congratulations on today's victory. It's as final as it is deserved."

Caesar turned to contemplate this figure. Like everyone, he was matted in dust; his helmet was badly dented and a cut on his arm was spilling blood onto his boots. After a moment Caesar realized this was Antonius speaking.

"Indeed it is final, Marce. The estimate is half of Pompey's troops have been killed. That would bring our losses to twenty thousand souls."

"Our losses, Caesar?"

"These were Romans, Marce. I have won the battle, but Rome has lost its bravest souls. Still," he added, pointing to corpses whose purple togas showed that they were one-time senators, "hoc voluerunt. They wanted this."

"And Fortuna, Caesar? What did she wish?" Antonius motioned to Caesar's left hand which he'd kept tightly clenched through the length of the battle. Hearing this question Caesar managed a smile. He opened his hand and displayed four knucklebones.

"You guessed correctly, Antonius. Fortuna, too, desired this outcome...."

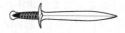

"Felix," a voice spoke, intruding on his reading, "Carolyn Manes will be arriving in the next ten minutes."

"That's right," Felix answered. He was seated at a counter and reading the *Lives of the Caesars.* "We're planning to play some Halo Ball."

"I will fix you a fruit shake and two protein biscuits. You could use caloric input and are partially dehydrated."

"That's a great idea, Mentor."

"The processing time is fifty-two seconds."

The Domestic System hummed as it set about this task. Closing his book, Felix waited for his snack, frowning because he knew what his mom would say. Mentor's prep time was slowly slipping. His processing speed was unimpressive and his software was outdated by sixteen years. They could upload the latest upgrades, but at the cost of altering Mentor's "profile." Fearing Mentor would seem like a stranger, Felix had insisted that they leave "him" be — to his mom's amusement. "I can't believe you're attached to a machine," she'd joked.

"Here's your snack," Mentor said. A panel opened and Felix removed its contents.

"Thanks, Mentor."

"You're welcome. Have you figured out that question yet?" He was referring to their discussion that morning, involving one of Johann Clavius's theories. Among his many breakthroughs, for which he'd won two Nobel Prizes, Clavius had uncovered the equations for time travel; this work had brought about the TPM, the device that had carried Felix back to the past. Intrigued by the scientist, Felix had been studying his work ever since.

"We were discussing butterfly effects," Felix said. He was looking out the window as he sipped his fruit shake.

"Clavius calls them temporal disruptions," Mentor observed. "By this he means the unseen effects when a subject from the future alters the course of the past."

"Right. Like if I travelled back in time and let off a bomb. But remind me what the question was?" Felix chewed his biscuit. A piece broke off and settled on the floor. Mentor's hygiene scan detected the crumb and zapped it with a low-watt laser.

"Can a temporal disruption be reversed? Clavius discusses this problem in the following manner. He imagines you were in the Boston airport, on September 11, 2001."

"He's referring to the 9/11 bombings," Felix said.

"That's correct. Clavius witnessed the religious wars, when the world was divided into *rats* and *theos*. 9/11 was the trigger event for this struggle. Returning to the example he uses, you see Mohamed Atta in the airport lounge."

"He was the chief hijacker."

"Yes. You break his hands so that he cannot work his mischief. But an instant later, Clavius supposes, you change your mind: your act might save the World Trade Center, but it will alter history, maybe for the worse. You decide it would be better for the attacks to occur. Clavius asks if there is something you can do. Can you reverse the effect of Mohamed Atta's broken hands?"

"Couldn't I hurry to the future then return to the past, to a time before I broke his hands? This way I can leave him be and allow him to accomplish his original plan."

"Clavius says no," Mentor answered. "When you broke his hands, this was registered in his timeframe. That means that the future you returned to would be the product of a past in which the towers weren't attacked."

"So there's no reversing a butterfly effect?" Felix sipped his shake again.

"There's one possibility," Mentor replied. "Clavius wrote that you can create a wormhole — this is a 'tunnel' linking two periods together, even if they are centuries apart. For as long as this wormhole is open, it will 'freeze' the past and stop it from changing the original future."

"Meaning?" Felix asked. He'd finished his shake. Placing the glass in a recess, he reached for a biscuit. There was a flash as the glass was sterilized.

"Let's get back to Mohamed Atta." As always, Mentor's tone was patient. "You regret that you have broken his hands. You build a wormhole and bring him to your future. Once there, you heal his hands so that he can hijack the plane. You return him to his past making use of the wormhole, to the moment when you first attacked him. If the wormhole is still open, the past hasn't changed from the moment you left it. Mohamed Atta can press on with his mission."

"I see," Felix said. He'd finished eating and spread his hands on the counter. Again there was a flash: the counter and his hands were instantly clean. "It's awful to think you couldn't interfere. But how do you build a wormhole?"

"If you create a field reversing the one that links you to the past, this would provide you with a bridge to the future. But first you would need a time machine; and we haven't constructed any such device."

As Felix thought of the TPM, a monitor came on and Carolyn's face appeared.

"Your guest has arrived," Mentor announced. "I must remind you, Felix, that you are scheduled to eat at 7:00 p.m. Your mother's shuttle will pick her up at nine. She cannot miss her flight to Ganymede."

"I'll remember," Felix said. "Want to come up?" he asked Carolyn. "You can snack before we play."

"I like playing when I'm hungry," she said. "Come to the courts. And prepare to lose."

She disconnected. While Felix should have smiled, he shivered instead. Her eyes had lost their shine and might have belonged to a killer.

Felix tore straight at the wall. Leaping at its surface, he climbed four steps and threw himself off, performing a backflip in the process. Tucking in mid-air, he landed in a crouch — his vacuum shoes took most of the shock. His tactic paid off: one ball hit the wall, while a second missed his head by an inch. The Halo balls scanned the space with their sensors and, detecting his coordinates, assailed him again. He rolled two times, regained his feet and performed a handstand on a ledge in the corner. With his feet against the wall and his hands on the ledge, he moved spider-like to dodge one ball, then its partner. Thrusting with his legs, he vaulted backwards, regained the floor, and hit the deck. For the third time in fifteen seconds, the balls failed to find their target.

"Ow! Stop!"

"Stop!" Felix cried, as the three-inch balls leapt forward again. Both stopped instantly and hung in midair. A light on each began to flash, a sign they'd entered sleep mode.

"That's five to one," Carolyn groaned, rubbing her arm where a ball had caught her.

"Had enough?" Felix gasped.

"For the moment, yeah. Let's take a breather." Still massaging her arm, Carolyn sat on the ledge. Remaining on his feet, Felix eyed her with concern.

At first sight she hadn't changed much since they'd met last year. Her blond hair was just as short, her height was the same, and her hazel stare was just as fierce, a perfect match for her sharply drawn chin. At the same time there *were* differences: she seemed more restless, more vulnerable, too. Although the last impression had to do with her colour: as Stephen had observed back on the transport, she was noticeably pale and also thinner.

"You've improved," she said grudgingly. A born competitor, she hated to lose.

"I've had time on my hands and practised a lot. And the moves you taught me come in handy. But it's you, as well. You're thinner and your eyes looked strained. I'll bet you're getting those headaches still."

"I'm 98 percent, according to Dr. Lee."

"You're seeing Dr. Lee?"

"Sure. He's still my family doctor, remember."

"Where are you seeing him? Here on-world or ..."

"Watch that," Carolyn warned.

Felix smiled. She was reminding him about his oath of silence, how he couldn't say anything about the TPM. As a general's daughter, she took such matters seriously.

But she wasn't just warning him to watch his tongue. She was also saying she didn't want to talk about "that." By "that" she meant their jump to the past. Their flight through time had just about killed them — Felix had been stabbed, while giant scorpions had almost eaten her alive. Whenever they'd discussed their "trip," she'd suffered nightmares for days on end. Several times she'd mentioned the Mem-rase program, much to Felix's disgust and distress.

"Did he say what it is?"

"It's an infection maybe. Or a residual effect of ... you know what."

"Don't worry. I won't spill any secrets. I'll keep them all *herkos odonton*."

"I thought we had an agreement," she said impatiently. "You promised not to use any Latin, remember?"

"It's not Latin, but Greek. It means the 'barrier of one's teeth' and is a way of promising to keep a secret."

"Latin, Greek," she sneered, "they're both the same."

Felix smiled weakly. It really was too bad. For a while after their return from the past, Carolyn had studied Latin with him, in exchange for lessons in karate and judo. They'd spent a lot of time together, on the Space Station, and, more often, on the Taylor terrace. They'd conjugated verbs, inflected nouns, and expanded her vocabulary. And then she'd stopped. It wasn't because the language bored her. On the contrary, she'd found it gorgeous and admired Cicero and Caesar. But the appeal of these authors had caused her concern: if she didn't watch out, she'd become "addicted" like Felix, with one foot in the modern world and one in the past. That struck her as unhealthy and she'd dropped the lessons.

"Stephen thinks you've got a screw loose," she went on. "He says you should leave your books and return to the real world."

"Those books saved his ass!" Felix snarled, startling Carolyn with the force of his anger. Her words pained him more than he could say. "If not for those texts, he'd have died from the plague! The same goes for everyone, your dad included. I'm amazed you've forgotten your debt to the past. But you're in very good company. If President Angstrom has his way, the Repository will be shuttered soon."

"Are you finished?" she asked, hardly impressed.

"No. I saw Stephen today. He wants you to wear something nice this evening. And he thinks you should alter your skin tone, too."

He and Carolyn glared at each other. Like most people she'd had her ERR extended and her features were perfectly controlled. At the same time, there was a glimmer of regret that she'd spoken so glibly of Felix's interests. She was fond of him, he knew, and was aware that they'd done amazing things together. But there was also her more practical bent. This was the part addressing him now.

"I've calculated the odds of the plague returning," she said. "Can you guess the results?"

"Tell me," Felix said.

"They're less than a billion to one. Our reliance on the past is virtually zero."

"And therefore we can ignore it. Is that what you're saying?"

"Yes. Look, the world was lucky that you speak Latin; we wouldn't be here if you didn't. But Pompey's dead, Spartacus is dead, Cicero's dead, and Rome is in ruins. If we're never threatened again, what's the use of studying something so ..."

"Meaningless?"

"Yes. Do you want to know what I think?"

"I don't know. Do I?"

"You can't go on like this. You'll drive yourself crazy. You'll be out of touch with everyone. As the president said today, we should try to be useful. That's why ..."

"Yeah?"

"You should submit to ERR. After that, we should have our memories deleted."

Felix smiled grimly. For the past six months, since Angstrom had broadened all ERR limits, Felix and Carolyn had debated the issue, especially when she'd adopted the upgrades. And now they were preparing to argue again, even though they were familiar with each other's views. Felix was about to say that their emotions meant a lot, and the past did too, while she was getting ready to "prove" that both were unimportant.

Before either could speak, the power failed. One moment there were lights; the next there was darkness. The Halo balls dropped to the floor and the vents grew silent.

"That's odd," Carolyn said. She was sitting nearby, but Felix couldn't see her.

"It's been happening a lot recently," he mused. "My transport failed when I was returning from Europe." He didn't add that he'd practically died of fright.

"There's a problem with the grid, I guess. Although it has so many fail-safes that stoppages shouldn't happen. Still, it had better return. I have to meet Stephen and his parents at seven."

"The failure won't last long," he answered tightly.

This second reference to Stephen upset him. It was bad enough she pooh-poohed his interests; her attraction to Stephen was the ultimate insult. Yes, the guy was bright, but he was also one-dimensional. He had no interest in anything that went beyond his ruthless logic.

At the same time, the question of ERR still nagged him. If he were to reduce the range of his emotions, would he appear more likeable in Carolyn's eyes?

"Your voice is strained," she said. "Is something wrong?"

"Nothing that concerns you," Felix replied. He was about to congratulate her for placing second in that contest when, as abruptly as they'd shut off, the lights came on. There was a hiss from the vents and the Halo balls were airborne.

Wordlessly, they left the court and entered a hallway whose lights were flashing on, one by one, in sequence. As they headed to the exit, the shadows in front of them dissolved. But as the lights returned, they affected Carolyn and helped her reach a firm decision. Something was coming, Felix could see. Sure enough, by the exit, she turned to face him.

"I just don't see the point," she said.

"I know."

"We had a great adventure," she continued. "But …"

"I understand," Felix said. "Don't worry. I'll remember it for both of us."

"Or we could forget it together."

"It's not in my nature to forget."

"I suppose it isn't. Well then …"

"Goodbye, Carolyn."

"Look after yourself."

She stepped outside and the door closed behind her. Felix shrugged and approached a stairwell. Of all the emotions plaguing him just then, envy was most powerful. He envied Carolyn her ability to forget. Maybe ERR and Mem-rase were worth looking into.

He didn't want to return upstairs. In a mood like this, he hated everything modern, Mentor included. Just then there was only one place to go, even if in some ways it was the source of all his troubles.

Chapter Three

*C*aesar stared at the people around him. He was walking to the Senate and the streets were crowded. The people watching him looked disappointed, angry even. Some were shouting, "Restore the Republic!" while others were crying, "Death to the king!"

He was feverish. He was also thinking about his wife, Calpurnia, who'd had an awful dream the night before. In it she'd held his corpse in her arms, bloody from a dozen wounds. When he'd calmed her, she'd reminded him of Spurrina's warning. The augur had told him to beware the Ides of March and now that very day had come. There were other omens, too, showing that his life was in danger. But he was Caesar. He didn't believe in dreams. Instead he listened only to … *Fortuna.*

It was only mid-March, but the day was hot. Mehercule! *The sun was bearing down on him with all the fury of a raging Gaul. The Via Flaminia wasn't shaded in this quarter. There was the Porticus Minucia over on his right, and the porticus belonging Jupiter and Juno, but these were located too far from the road. Dust was in the air and the crowd was suffocating. It was lucky he was nearing the Theatre of Pompey. This is where the senate would meet while the Curia Julia was under construction.*

Poor Pompey, he mused. Yes, they'd been enemies; if he'd lost at Pharsalus, Pompey would have killed him. At the same time, he'd been a good friend once and his murder in Egypt was nothing short of tragic. Where was Pompey now? At rest and indifferent to all earthly matters? Or was he angry and wishing ill on Caesar?

"Down with Caesar!" someone yelled from nearby. Because of his fever, he heard these words as if he were submerged; unfortunately they were still audible. He sighed. Did people think he was scheming to be king? Did they think he enjoyed ruling over the city? No! A thousand times no! He would give up all his power if the Romans would behave. But they were too contentious to live in peace for long. That's why he had to sit on their heads, until he knew they wouldn't start fighting again.

Pompey's Theatre was coming up. A group of senators was standing before its entrance, Casca, Cassius, Galba, and others. He shivered slightly. This band had him nervous. They'd protested his rule and didn't wish him well. Maybe Calpurnia was right and he was in danger. Perhaps he should retreat and meet these dogs when he was stronger. His fingers grabbed his knucklebones, to determine what Fortuna thought.

As his fingers grazed the astragali, another face appeared. Brutus, thank goodness. A dignified, polite young man, he'd be sure to safeguard Caesar. He waved to the leader. Caesar waved back. He abandoned the astragali and hastened forward, sure that Brutus was a better protector than Fortuna.

The sun was bright and blinded him slightly.

A burst of music broke in on Felix. The sound was scratchy, but he recognized the piece: Bach's 2nd Brandenburg Concerto. He set his book down and pushed back the chair. Twenty metres off, his dad was wrestling with a ladder by a shelf. Because the shelves rolled on for thirty metres and almost touched the elevated ceiling, the ladder was handy, never mind that it would jam against the sliding bar. That had happened now and his dad was trying to unstick it.

"Do you need help?" Felix asked, making his way over. He had to yell over the music.

"That's alright. I can manage. Continue reading."

"I could use a break." That was true. Felix was feeling tense after hearing Angstrom's speech and knowing it was quits with Carolyn. At the same time he was trying not to think of his mother. She was leaving that night and he dreaded her departure. He'd been reading to distract himself, but the tactic wasn't working.

"Where are you in the text?" his father asked, his head bobbing in time to the music.

"Caesar's about to die. Are you sure you can manage?"

"I'm fine. But tell me. When Caesar met his assassins, did he guess what they were planning? Did he know that death was lying in wait?"

"I don't think he would have joined them if he had."

"That's true," his father mused, freeing the ladder. "But after Pharsalus I think his feelings changed. The battle set Rome on an even keel. It was less corrupt, more stable, too. Caesar had lots of blood on his hands, Roman blood at that, but the city was renewed. With his job accomplished, he could die in peace."

Felix was puzzled by his father's comment. He was going to ask him to be more specific, when again the sliding ladder stuck. At the same time a pencil fell to the floor and rolled beneath a shelf. As his father cursed, Felix smiled. In a world whose shape was always changing, his dad was a factor that remained the same.

Most adults liked to alter their hair, modify their bodies, and vary their clothes to suit the day's tastes. When Angstrom changed the ERR strictures, everyone took these protocols on. When new supplements appeared, new games, new gadgets, new conveniences, new fashions, new habits, or new uploads, everybody would embrace this "progress" except his father. He stuck with his routines, his books, and music, his Zacron suits and pencil stubs. While the world moved faster, he continued at the same pace, deliberate, consistent, and easy-going.

No, that wasn't quite true. He'd changed a bit in recent months, on account of the plague. Mr. Taylor had been its victim and actually died. Felix had saved him by jumping back in time and handing him the cure before the plague could kill him. But his dad had been ambivalent. As he'd confessed weeks later, he hadn't been despondent at death's door. He'd hated the idea of leaving his family, but been relieved to leave a world that struck him as empty.

He was more frail now, and angrier, too. Tiny incidents could set him cursing and waving his pencil about like a dagger. Even the Repository and Bach barely soothed him these days.

"Could you hand me that book?" his father said. He was standing on the ladder and motioning to a pile. "The big one with the glossy cover."

"What book is this?" Felix asked, as he examined the cover's English title: *Cuisine of Provence*. He handed the heavy tome to his dad. "Do we have enough space to save cookbooks now? Mentor can track these recipes down."

"It's not the recipes that interest me," Mr. Taylor replied, "but the book's implications." He shelved the book and descended the ladder, speaking as he picked his way down. "As late as 2083, people still fixed meals for themselves. Domestic units were very rare. People ate outside the house, in something called a restaurant, or bought ingredients and cooked these at home, in an oven they controlled themselves. It was a common practice in the recent past."

"What a strange idea," Felix said.

"And there was more," his father added. "Look." He stooped and retrieved four more books from the floor. "Here's a book on sewing. Imagine. Some people actually sewed their clothes. And here's one on car repairs and another on plumbing. And here's one that teaches you to play a piano. Can you imagine? Not only did people listen to music; some were able to play it themselves. When I think …"

He couldn't finish. Setting the books down, he went to his desk. Before following him, Felix gazed around. The Repository was located in a steel-girder building, built as a department store in the late nineteenth century. People had assembled here to buy clothes, perfumes, and household goods; on a holiday called Christmas they had packed the aisles. Now these aisles were packed with books. Seven centuries of tomes filled its shelves, which stretched as far as the eye could see. When Felix roamed its hollows, he could practically hear the books talking, pleading to have their contents saved and promising in exchange to share their secrets.

While he'd spent a lot of time in this space, it was only recently, because of his dad's weakness, that he'd really come to know it well. He'd wandered each section a million times, memorized titles by the tens of thousands and could track down materials with blinding speed. Having scoured out every nook and cranny, he knew the Repository inside out.

With the exception of the storage room. In the building's northwest corner, there was a tiny space with an old-fashioned lock. When Felix asked his dad about it, he answered that the room was where he kept the family skeletons, ones that he was best off forgetting. Felix didn't care. There was plenty of other stuff to hold his interest. Each day introduced him to a thousand new titles.

But his dad was waiting. Felix hurried down the aisle toward his desk. As he emerged from the shelving, a statue hailed him — the goddess Diana. Felix threw her a smile, mindful that she'd saved him from the past last year.

He sat at the desk. He'd barely settled down when an object drew his eye. His smile faded and he clenched his teeth. An e-notice was hovering just out of reach. It bore a 3-D image of the presidential seal and paraded words like "Eviction, "Efficiencies," and "Waste." He turned to his father who was sprawled out in an armchair.

"I'm sorry, Felix," he said, "I shouldn't be so gruff. These days I just can't help myself. Objects like that cookbook seem like such a … reproach. Not to mention crap like that." He pointed to the notice.

Felix nodded sympathetically "Two teas," he spoke into a cube on the desk. "Milk, no sugar." He glanced back at his dad. "What do you mean by a reproach?"

"We're so removed from what we used to be." His father sighed and squirmed in his chair. "Suetonius' day was admittedly rough. But at least he saw humans at their best. They were generous, courageous, idealistic, and enduring. Our age is the opposite. We're blessed with affluence and would never hurt our neighbours. Yet we're unfeeling and uninterested in anything other than the present. Is this the price we pay for progress? We can't have comfort without losing our best instincts?"

His words didn't come as a surprise; after all, he'd been expressing such opinions for years. The difference now was that his mood was bleak. Whereas formerly he'd always spoken with humour, as well as hope, his tone these days was only despondent. The fluttering e-notice only mocked him further.

A light flashed once and a whistle sounded. Approaching a panel that stood waist-high, Felix tugged it open. Behind it were two cups of tea. Removing these, he handed one to this father. He then returned to his chair and blew on his drink.

"When I was young, *fili mi*," his father continued, "the violence of the past used to make me tremble. I pitied the Romans when the Vandals smashed their city, the Aztecs when the Spanish crushed them like ants, the victims of the two World Wars, the *rats* who died at the hands of the *theos* and the *theos* whom the *rats* extinguished. It reassured me, too, to know that I would never see such acts committed, that art, books, and music would never die before my eyes. And yet, for all our comfort, no, *because* of our comforts, the barbarians are at the gates again."

"Barbarians?" Felix asked. As he spoke, the concerto hit a climax in the background.

"There are different types," his father said, sipping from his cup. "Some are louts toting guns and knives. Others are soft-spoken and possess the smartest minds you'll ever meet. They're more dangerous than the first variety. With their technology and gadgets, they've made all culture obsolete and altered the very thrust of our souls. As for the past ..." He pointed to the e-notice. Its presidential seal was like a slap in the face.

Felix frowned as he sipped his tea. He was thinking how Stephen had won Carolyn over. He'd never see her again, would he? His eccentricities had chased her off.

As if sensing his tension, Mr. Taylor smiled whimsically. Reaching over, he squeezed Felix's hand.

"Enough of that," he said. "Let's go home and talk to your mother. When she leaves tonight, we won't see her for a while. Let's enjoy the evening and shelve our gloomy thoughts."

Climbing to his feet, his dad began shutting the Repository down. He flicked a long series of switches and, as the ceiling lights went off, successive aisles went black. Watching the shadows enfold the books, Felix thought they captured all his father's fears. The present was eating into the past, so thoroughly that no trace of it would survive into the future.

Chapter Four

"How pretty the earth is," Mrs. Taylor gushed. "I've seen this view a thousand times yet it never fails to thrill me."

"It is beautiful," her husband agreed.

"The strangest part about working off-world," Mrs. Taylor went on, "is that the farther off you are from Earth, the less unique it seems. From Ganymede it's like another rock in space. You'd never guess it was home to thinking creatures like us."

"How do you do it?" Mr. Taylor said, "If I were standing on Ganymede, I'd miss Earth so badly. I couldn't be away from it for three long months. Why are you laughing?"

"Because you of all people have good reason to leave. It really is funny. You hate this world, yet you insist on staying."

"I have to stay. Who else will keep these people honest? Besides Felix, that is."

Felix started when he heard his name. He'd been staring out the window at the start of outer space. They were in a private shuttle, travelling to the Space Hub, which was floating in the Earth's exosphere.

The Earth. It was poised beneath Felix's feet, and, for all its vastness, looked strangely frail. Surrounded by a tract of space, it seemed on the verge of suffering some crisis. Maybe a comet would strike from out of the blue, cosmic rays would burn it to cinders, or another plague would rear its head and bring people to their knees. Would he like that? Would he like its masses to be hammered again, only this time no one would come to the rescue? As his family floated safely on high, Siegfried Angstrom would sicken, Stephen Gowan, too, the general, Carolyn …

No. Not Carolyn. The thought of something hurting her…

"You're very quiet," his mother said.

Felix merely smiled. A week ago there'd been a "leak" on Ganymede and all its housing had been badly affected. CosmoComm needed someone to supervise on site, and by "someone" they meant Mrs. Taylor. She'd booked a seat on the next heavy transport and the day of her departure had finally come, much to Felix's disappointment. He liked having his mother home. Her comfort with technology balanced out his dad's obsession with the past. She'd be gone three months and the house would seem empty.

"What'll you do while I'm away?"

"I'll read Tacitus," Felix answered, "and some more recent authors. The twenty-first century interests me; the way religion and technology went to war with each other."

"That period reminds me of Rome's last days," his dad broke in. "We should read Procopius of Caesarea. He writes about barbarians and the city's final gasps."

"That sounds cheerful," Mrs. Taylor joked.

"And I'll hunt for more books," Felix added, before his dad could mention the Repository and how the new barbarians were plotting to close it. "Cookbooks in particular."

"Cookbooks?" Mrs. Taylor asked. "What are those?"

"It's a joke," Felix answered, winking at his father. While his mother believed in her husband's project, she knew nothing about history. "I was born in 2170," she always argued. "I remember events from my own day and not much more." Her family's talk of Julius Caesar, Pericles, Napoleon, and Karl Marx, and events and figures closer to the present, Clavius, Xiu, Goldberg, *rats* and *theos*; these baffled her in much the same way that her talk of zero gravity torque mystified Felix.

Felix had once asked his mom what had drawn her to his father. Their perspectives were different, their tastes were different, their jobs were different, *they* were different. Why had she thought their marriage would work?

"I may not know about the past," she'd answered, pausing briefly to consider his question, "but I respect it deeply. It comforts me to know that, while I construct my units, someone is keeping our history alive. Nowadays everyone knows math and physics. Only rare birds, like your father and you, have studied languages from earlier times. How couldn't I fall for such a man? The same way an engineer will one day lose her heart to you."

Felix knew it hadn't been quite like that. When his mom had met his father, she'd been equipped with ERR. Without it, she maintained, she couldn't perform her job. Off-world housing had to be perfect. If the O_2 flow was off by one percent or the vacuum seals slipped by even a micron, people would die. When she handled these jobs, she had to focus. She couldn't dwell on anything but the task at hand because for a working engineer, emotions could be lethal.

But to value Mr. Taylor, her feelings couldn't be "filtered." Suspicious as he was of ERR, he'd never have assumed it just for her, and never have befriended her if she'd "worn" it all the time. At the start of their relationship, they'd discussed this subject bitterly and come within a hair of splitting up. Finally they'd brokered a compromise. When her job required it, her ERR was on; when her family beckoned, it was disengaged. After that, the pair had gotten along and been happily married for the longest time.

Only once had Felix seen her in ERR mode. He'd been five years old. An emergency had come up and she'd installed the filter before leaving home. Her demeanour had been chilling. Felix remembered the look in her eye, the dull, cold glaze of her brain at work, unhindered by fear, sadness, or affection. If Felix had been killed in front of her eyes, she could have ignored his death and continued working. It had taken him weeks to get over this trauma and to see her as his mom again and not as some cyborg.

"Hello there!" a voice broke in. "I hope I'm not intruding?"

Felix glanced round in confusion. Like both his parents, he cracked a smile when he spied Professor MacPherson on a Teledata screen. Besides the Taylors, MacPherson was the only man alive who knew Latin, Greek, and other foreign languages, as well as history, art, and culture. He was part of the TPM project and had helped Felix out the previous year. Not only had the professor been in touch since then, but he'd befriended the older Taylors, too. They'd had him over for dinner often, and Felix and his dad would sometimes meet him for lunch. MacPherson was the cheerful sort and never failed to raise the family's spirits.

"You're never intruding, Ewan," Mrs. Taylor said. "You should know that by now."

"I'm a slow learner," the professor joked, "but I did remember that you're leaving tonight. I wanted to wish you a very safe trip. I also wanted to remind the Taylor men that we must meet while you're frolicking on Ganymede. This will keep your boys from getting into mischief. Do you hear me, Eric?"

"Loud and clear," Mr. Taylor replied. For the first time that day, he was smiling widely. "We'll be sure to take you up on your offer. Felix is reading Suetonius and he'd love to hear what you make of the Caesars."

"And I would love to hear what he thinks. We three must form a triumvirate soon."

"Very soon," Felix and his father agreed.

"In that case, *pax vobiscum*."

A second later, his face was gone. The Taylors were beaming still and thinking they were lucky to have such a friend.

"We're almost there," Mrs. Taylor observed, breaking the silence. "The station looks spectacular if I say so myself."

She was glancing at a wheel-shaped structure whose diameter was eight kilometres in length. At the Space Hub's centre was a Welcome Hall; radiating outward were twelve passageways, the "spokes" on this orbiting wheel. Each spoke led to a docking port where various heavy transports lay waiting; from the Hub they would fly to their off-world destinations. With its Class P solar panels, totalium joints and thrusters neutralizing orbit decay, the Hub was a monument to human daring.

"It's still working," Mrs. Taylor said, pointing out a house-sized device that resembled a giant honeycomb forged from metal. This object was a CO_2 filter that enabled people on the Hub to breathe. It was Mrs. Taylor's addition to the project.

"You must be proud your work lets people travel in space," Felix said, with a note of awe. The shuttle was approaching a dock on the Hub; the closer they drew to the structure, the more majestic it seemed.

"I am proud," his mom admitted. "But engineering is a means to an end. And the end is what the two of you do, history, literature, that sort of thing. Besides, your dad contributed to this project, too —"

She was interrupted by a low-pitched hum. A magnetic field had embraced the shuttle and was guiding its bulk toward a space on the dock. At the same time a Greeting Tube attached itself to the shuttle's exit and, with a hiss that sounded like a dragon exhaling, joined the craft and the Hub's exterior. A voice announced that the shuttle had docked and they could exit safely.

Felix's parents entered a hallway. They walked arm-in-arm and chatted together. Felix followed, his eyes studying the scene. The spoke they were in had see-through panels and offered a stunning view outside. Drones were everywhere, assisting people with their baggage: two were handling his mother's trunk. Travel Bots were scanning passengers' eyes and directing them to their proper port. The place was beautiful and stunningly efficient, but, as was the case with modern spaces, had very little soul.

No. That wasn't quite true. The passageway had ended and they were entering the Welcome Hall. In addition to its vaulted ceiling, Titex dome, and high-tech comforts, the hall offered something else. At its centre, on a piece of rock, was a statue of Poseidon, god of the seas. The figure was three metres high, bearded, naked, and wielding a trident. It was twenty-three centuries old at least, yet its marble hadn't lost its shine and was carved with such breathtaking skill that the god seemed on the verge of moving. As his dad had predicted when he'd proposed this statue to the Space Hub's builders, it lent the hall both dignity and warmth. It was appropriate, too, that this god of the seas should be the custodian of outer space.

As Felix stood admiring this work, he saw that his dad was consulting a drone to check if the transport was leaving on time. Seeing he was busy, Mrs. Taylor left his side and walked over to Felix. As she drew in close, her face betrayed a look of worry.

"I have to make this quick," she whispered, pointing to her husband who'd finished with the drone. "I'd rather not be leaving home, but I don't have any choice in the matter. While I'm gone, I want you to watch your father. I hate to say this, but his mood is black and he could do something desperate."

That said, she gave Felix a kiss, smiled widely and rejoined her husband, clasping his hand in hers as if everything were normal.

They were returning from the Space Hub. They'd said goodbye to Mrs. Taylor, who'd cried while kissing them both farewell. Felix had managed to hide his tears, but just. His mom had headed to the heavy transport where (he assumed) she'd engaged her ERR and put an end to her sadness.

Felix and his dad were riding in silence. They were thinking how empty their house would be, even as they took in the beautiful view. The shuttle was flying toward the Earth, whose surface was spread out wide before them. Its colours were magnificent, a blend of greens, browns, and blues. The lights, too, were breathtaking, the way they were sprinkled across each continent, like icing on a wedding cake. Eyeing the planet, Felix thought it looked old. Through the course of its history it had witnessed so much, the birth of the seas, continental drift, the start of life, the dinosaurs' extinction. Nothing could unfold that would take it by surprise, not even the moment of its own demise. "You miss your mom already?" it asked. "Don't worry. The feeling will pass. Like everything else."

Felix was going to wink in reply when, abruptly, the lights went dark. As if a veil had been drawn across the face of North America, every sign of modern times went black, only to return a few seconds later.

Felix looked at his dad and shivered slightly. In contrast to his earlier gloom, his dad was grinning, like someone who's glimpsed a rare and beautiful sunset.

Chapter Five

He was seated in an alcove in Pompey's Theatre. Senators surrounded him and were taking up his elbow room. He barely had any space to breathe. One grabbed his toga. When he told him to let go, the figure drew a knife. As if that were a signal, the other senators brandished knives, as well. Their eyes were cold and spitting death. Had all of them undergone ERR? But how could that be? There was no ERR in ancient Rome and...? The senators stared and shook the alcove with their laughter.

Felix started and opened his eyes. He'd been dreaming. The strange part was his room *was* shaking and a roar-like laughter filled his ears. No, it wasn't a roar so much as an insistent buzzing, as if bees had constructed a hive in their unit. He sat up straight and glanced around. The dark enfolded him because his night light was off. How…?

"Mentor! What's happening?" he cried, struggling with his pants and shirt.

No answer. Felix shivered slightly. It didn't worry him that the lights were off — the power had probably failed again — but the auxiliary cells should have kicked in. The only way these could fail was if Mentor was disabled and why would anyone…?

Felix blanched. This had happened before. Last year, when the plague was raging, a Medevac had broken into the house, "murdered" Mentor and snatched Felix away. There'd been a reason then; there was a reason now.

"What's going on? You have no right…!"

That was his father speaking! His voice was raised and he sounded angry. Running from his bedroom, Felix rushed down a hallway.

"Citizen 967597102-364," a metallic voice rang out. "We are arresting you, under Section 17A of the Global Criminal Code!"

"Dad!" Felix called. He'd reached the living room. Hovering outside the picture window and blocking the view of the skyline, three cruisers had their flashers on. An ultrasound wand had cut the glass on the windows and two Enforcement Drones had entered the unit. They were four feet high, cylindrically shaped, and bristling all over with switches and sensors. They were floating waist-high and flashing beams of light. They also had their stun-rods out; these could deliver a powerful shock.

Mr. Taylor was in a sleep suit. His feet were bare, his hair was a mess, and his hands were shielding his eyes from the lights. He glanced Felix's way.

"Go to your room, *fili mi*. There's been a mistake. Did you hear me?" he told the drones. "There's been a mistake!"

"Citizen 967597102-364," the voice repeated dully, "we are arresting you, under Section 17A of the Global Criminal Code. You are not entitled to legal counsel and will be kept in captivity until further notice...."

"This is nonsense!" Mr. Taylor cried. More EDs streamed into the room along with a floating one-man stretcher, its clear lid open and arms upraised. "Stay away!" he threatened, backing into a book case.

"You heard him!" Felix yelled. Groping in the dark, he found a stone that his mother had brought from Ganymede. It was rough and weighed a kilo at least. As an ED made its stun-rod ready, he hurled the stone and heard it strike the drone's surface.

The machine issued a high-pitched shriek. The other drones swarmed Mr. Taylor and there was a *zssst* sound as a stun-rod made contact. His dad's eyes widened and his body slumped forward as the arms from the stretcher reeled him into its hollows. Felix wanted to help, but he himself was under attack. The drones were turning their sights on him.

"Citizen 967597102-366," one spoke. "We are arresting you, under Section 12G of the Secrecy Act. You are not entitled —"

It couldn't finish. The family Entertainment Complex lay to Felix's right. He kicked it over and detached its metal tripod — it was two feet long and very solid. Swinging it hard, he hit the drone above its "neck" and crushed its CPU. There was a squawk as the drone shook out of control and knocked into the other EDs, blocking their efforts to apprehend Felix. Making use of this chaos, he ran to his room and sealed its heavy door behind him. Locating the lock's circuit, he slammed it with the tripod and saw a blue flame emerge. He smiled in satisfaction. The lock was "non-negotiable" for the next few minutes.

He wondered what his next step was. He wanted to rescue his father, right? That meant handling the drones, hijacking a cruiser, and piloting the craft to a safe location. The task was hard, impossible, even. "So what are you waiting for?" he asked aloud.

He drew near the window. Swinging the tripod, he slammed it into the pane several times in rapid succession. The Duroplex couldn't take these blows. It cracked then smashed into a million fragments. Impressed with this destruction, Felix laughed aloud.

Tucking the tripod into his pants, he stepped onto the window frame and ignored the drop below. He leapt onto a nearby wall. It marked the east side of the terrace, which, with its trees, shrubbery, and bust of old poets, was in some ways the heart of the Taylor household. Felix had spent long hours here, reading and discussing texts with his father. And Carolyn had learned Latin here.

But never mind that. Felix proceeded along the wall until he was immediately below a security cruiser. His timing was perfect. The stretcher bearing his dad was being loaded on board, escorted by a dozen EDs. Gripping the craft's landing gear, Felix swung himself upward and slammed into the foremost drone. Caught off guard, it flew off at an angle and struck a window on the floor above. Before the other EDs could react, Felix shoved the stretcher onto the craft.

A drone on board took its stun-rod out. Felix ducked and swung the tripod hard. Again he struck its CPU and utterly crushed it. The drone sputtered briefly and went offline.

A drone outside tried to enter the cruiser, but Felix engaged a switch by the exit. With a whine of power, the door slid closed. He dodged around the stretcher, ignoring his dad's pallor, and twisted his way to the ship's controls, his tripod raised in case the "pilot" attacked. Before he reached the cab, there was a rush of movement.

Six BISDMs lunged out — Brain Interference Signal Delivery Mechanisms. They were fist-sized spheres equipped with neuron disruptors. Felix dodged two spinning orbs and swung out at a third.

It was hopeless. Avoiding the tripod easily, the orbs closed in. A blue wave erupted from their surface "bristles." It swept over Felix, freezing his muscles and disabling his senses. There was a *whoosh* in his ears, the lights grew blurry, and he slumped against the stretcher with his dad. A horrible taste filled his mouth, metallic and salty. Was that blood? Who would have known?

Keep going! a voice in his skull kept shrieking. *Stand up! Don't surrender!* But a veil took shape, impossibly black, and settled about him like a favourite blanket.

Within seconds he was lost within its endless folds.

"You can open your eyes," a voice addressed him. It was familiar-sounding, but impatient now. "All your readings are normal, Felix. Stop wasting time and look at me."

Felix forced his eyes open and shook his head. A flat, grey ceiling was poised above him, its dullness barely brightened by a rust-coloured light.

"That's better. Now sit up."

With a colossal effort, he sat himself straight. He was in some sort of cell. If he jumped, his head would strike the ceiling, while the walls were close and tomb-like. He was lying on a bench that was fixed to one wall; in front of him was a picture window.

General Manes was staring in; he was Carolyn's father. More to the point, he ran the TPM and had worked with Felix the previous year. While he found Felix odd, he'd always been friendly. Just then, however, there was nothing friendly about him.

"Where's my father?" Felix groaned. "Why did you arrest him?"

"I'll ask the questions," the general growled. His green eyes studied Felix coldly. It was clear from his hard-set features that, like Carolyn, his ERR had been upgraded. Formerly quite personable, he now had all the warmth of a service drone.

"There's been a mistake —" Felix started to say.

"At 3:04 a.m.," the general barked, "someone broke into the Station and made a time projection."

"Hang on," Felix said, holding up a hand. His head was ringing still. "Are you saying someone's gone back in time?"

"That's exactly what I'm saying. Don't tell me this is news to you."

"This is crazy ..." Felix began. Despite his grogginess, he was growing impatient.

Cutting him short, the general listed the facts. An unauthorized "guest" had entered the Station and aimed a gun at Dr. Lee, the TPM's chief scientist. Against his will, Dr. Lee had charged a range of ancient landmarks, creating time portals in all of them. With this done, he'd been forced to enter four dates into the TPM's console. The "guest" had then led a third party forward, a masked figure roughly the size of a child. Again, at the threat of being shot, Dr. Lee had planted a tracer in this "child": it was programmed with the same four dates as the ones in the console. The "child" had stepped into the TPM and been swept to the first date entered, dissolving like an object that had been struck by a laser. The "guest" had knocked Dr. Lee unconscious, abandoned the Station, and flown back to Earth.

"All of this," the general added, "was beautifully planned. Those blackouts we've experienced these last two weeks? This 'guest' was responsible. He's been siphoning off power to make this time jump possible."

"Even so," Felix said, "I still don't see how my dad's involved. Nothing you've said incriminates him … or me."

"A CosmoComm craft went missing last night," the general went on, with a smile so sharp he might have used it to shave. "It was the one your family took to the Space Hub. Its log says it left your home at 1:13 a.m. and flew directly to the TPM. Some three hours later, it returned to your place…."

"What?" Felix cried.

"Zacron fibres were left in the Station — these come from the suit that the intruder was wearing. I made a few inquiries. Do you know how many people dress in Zacron? Remarkably few. I discovered your father's name was among them."

Felix's mouth was open, but he didn't dare speak. How often had his mother begged her husband to change his taste in fashion?

"And this happened to slip from one of his pockets." The general held up an object. "There aren't a lot of people who write with pencils these days. Again, I discovered your father does. Putting all these facts together, the shuttle, the suit, and the tell-tale pencil, I assembled holograms of possible suspects. Among them was your dad's. When Dr. Lee spied his portrait, he identified your dad as his attacker."

"That's impossible!"

"Are you calling Dr. Lee a liar?"

"No, I mean ..." Felix was thunderstruck. This didn't make sense. His dad collected books. He wasn't able to cause blackouts or hijack shuttles. As for the TPM, he didn't even know the facility existed!

"I know what you're thinking," the general crooned. "Your dad loves books and is hopeless with technology. So it might interest you to know that he's a first-rate engineer. With his training, such stunts would be a piece of cake."

"This is insane!"

"I can show you his diploma," the general snapped. "But never mind that. What bothers me is how he knew about our project. But I think I've got that figured out. You're familiar with the TPM. You either told your dad about it —."

"I did no such thing!" Felix interrupted.

"— or you divulged it indirectly, through a careless remark. One way or another, you gave him ideas," the general went on calmly. "And once the seed caught fire, he organized this venture."

Why, Felix wondered, *why would his dad...?*

Again the general was ahead of him. "You're wondering what he's up to, right? The answer's pretty simple. He's a scholar, addicted to ancient stuff. So he's probably chasing some hidden text, monument, or artifact. That 'child' he dispatched? If this 'kid' buried some precious relic in a cave or pit or somewhere safe, your dad could dig it up right now and study it first-hand. He's conducting research, in other words, and at other times I wouldn't give a damn, only he's broken the law, threatened violence, breached our security, and consumed mass quantities of power ..."

The general's rant continued, but Felix wasn't listening. His mind was awhirl. His father was an engineer. Who could have known? And the shuttle, the pencil stub, the Zacron suit, as well as Dr. Lee's ID: all of these pointed to his father's guilt. Except that Felix had never mentioned the Station, nor had he referred to it even in passing. So how...?

Wait. There was the ring that Spartacus had given him. While Felix seldom wore it, his dad had spied it some months back and asked where it had come from. Felix had said it was from Italy, but his dad might have guessed there was more to the tale. There was also the dust that Mentor had scanned. Felix had brought it back from the past and Mentor had dated it to Roman times. Had his dad picked up on this information?

Felix squinted hard. There was something else. Last year he'd been "bumped" to 2001. His only way back to 2213 had been the portal in a temple that his dad would excavate in 2203. Unfortunately, Felix had left a laptop behind. If his dad had found it in the course of his dig, he'd have wondered what a laptop was doing on a site that had been buried for over two thousand years. Along with the dust and Spartacus's ring, it might have led him to infer the TPM's existence. Finally, Felix had often met Carolyn at the Station. If his dad had slipped a tracker in his clothes, he could have learned of the TPM's location.

So maybe his dad had put two and two together. And maybe he'd siphoned power through those mini blackouts, piloted the shuttle to the TPM, and dispatched that "child" back in time. The question remained … why? Why on earth had he gone to such lengths? Was this really part of some "research project," as the general maintained? But what was he researching? And why keep Felix in the dark? Why use this so-called child instead of his son, who knew Latin and could navigate the past more effectively? Come to think of it, why hadn't his father worn a mask? Why had he revealed his face to the doctor and multiplied the odds of getting caught?

Unless …

Felix remembered his mom's parting words, how she felt her husband could do something desperate. His face turned pale.

"What's the matter?" the general sneered. "Is your conscience troubling you? Is there something you'd like to tell me now that the horse has left the stable?"

Felix didn't hear him. He was thinking how bitter his father was, that the world had turned its back on the past, and the Repository was in danger of being closed. Was he angry enough to want to teach it a lesson?

"Tell me about the dates," he urged the general.

"Dates? What dates?" the general asked, surprised by Felix's question.

"The ones entered into the TPM's console. What was the 'child's' first destination?"

"You don't know?" the general jeered.

"Tell me!" Felix roared. "This could be serious!"

The general glared at him, puzzled by his anger. At the same time something made him uneasy. Unfolding his arms, he cleared his throat and spoke. "The first date was May 30, 71 BCE. The place was Cremona, the temple of Belenus. What's the matter? You look like you're about to be sick."

Felix was staring hard at the general. His eyes said everything, but he set it in words. "I hate to say this but we're in serious danger."

"Come on," the general said. "What sort of danger?"

"The return of the plague," Felix said. "Only this time there won't be any possible cure."

Chapter Six

"Tell the doctor what you told me. Take it from the top."

Felix was seated in the station's viewing section. Behind him was a window looking onto the stars. With him were the general and Dr. Lee. All three were drinking tea, as if they were friends taking an afternoon break. The one detail hinting that this exchange wasn't friendly was the trio of drones surrounding the table. The general didn't trust Felix and was taking no chances.

"That 'child' who's jumped to the past. His intentions are deadly."

"What makes you say that?" Dr. Lee asked. "This is a strange plot, yes, but that doesn't mean it's dangerous. Your father's doing some research, that's all. While I consider him reckless, I'm sure he means no harm." He sipped his tea. He'd always been a quiet, dignified man, but now he had a sad dimension, despite his ERR. This was because of the loss he'd sustained. While Felix had been able to stop the plague, he couldn't rescue all its victims and across the globe thousands had perished. Dr. Lee's son had been among the dead.

"It's the date," Felix said. "When Carolyn and I went back last year, our entry date was June 15, 71 BCE. Of all the times this 'child' could jump to, why's his date so close to ours? And his destination is Cremona, in Cisalpine Gaul."

"So?"

"It's Aceticus' hometown."

"He wrote about the *lupus ridens*," the general said.

"I remember Aceticus," the doctor said. "I don't see —"

"Look," Felix said, with a note of impatience, "my dad found out about the TPM — how, I don't know. He put me on to Aceticus, remember? So he knows the importance of the *lupus ridens*. Now he's sent this 'child' to Aceticus' town around the time I travelled to the past last year."

"Yes," the doctor mused. The implications were trickling in.

"He didn't trust me with this task," Felix continued, "because it was something he knew I'd never agree to. And he didn't wear a mask when he held you up because he knew it wouldn't matter if his plan succeeded."

"Succeeded how?" the doctor asked. His strangled tone suggested he knew the answer already.

"For his own crazy reasons, he wants the plague to return. That means stopping Aceticus from writing his book. If he can't write it, I can't read it. If I can't read it, the plague will rage. So that 'child' is after Aceticus. Who he is, I have no idea. But if he finds his target, all of us will die. And when I say all of us, I mean every living soul."

"Why kill everyone?" the general asked. Through his ERR, a glimmer of rage was visible. "He doesn't care about his wife and son?"

"He thinks it will claim a small number of lives. If a thousand die, or even a million, that's a price worth paying if we mend their ways. He doesn't know, the way I do, that the plague will kill every human at large and no one, I mean no one, will escape with their life."

Dr. Lee was about to sip his tea. He stopped in mid-course, his hand suddenly shaking. Tea spilled all over and he winced as if in pain. There was a flash as a hygiene system dealt with the mess.

"My apologies," the doctor spoke. "The attack last night is affecting my nerves."

"That's all right," the general said. He was frowning hard and busy thinking. "Let's assume you're right, Felix. Why were four dates entered into the TPM as well as into the 'child's' blood? Besides his trip to 71 BCE, the 'kid' is scheduled to travel to Stockholm in 2111, then to Alexandria in 48 BCE. We haven't retrieved the fourth date from the console. It's been coded and is difficult to read."

"Maybe these are alternate targets. If the 'child' fails the first time, he'll have three more options. But we'll figure them out later. Right now, Aceticus is our main concern."

"What do you suggest?" Dr. Lee asked. He could barely breathe and spoke with effort.

"Send me to the past, to intercept this 'child.' I'll warn Aceticus or try to protect him."

"We could send you to May 29th," the general said. "You could find Aceticus and —"

"No," Felix cut in. "That 'child' is in the wrong place. Aceticus isn't in Cremona."

"But you said it was his hometown," the doctor protested.

"It is, but he's not there. He's visiting Rome."

"How do you know?" the general demanded.

"Because Carolyn and I saw him there. We were in a stadium and Aceticus happened along — this was on June sixteenth. He'd been in Rome awhile, I'm sure. The 'kid' won't find him in Cremona, believe me."

The general looked at Felix. Felix returned his glance then exchanged looks with the doctor. The trio continuing trading stares until the general slapped the table and set the teacups rattling.

A decision had been reached. Felix was off.

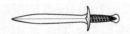

"How are you feeling?" Dr. Lee asked.

"Groggy," Felix admitted.

"Don't worry. You'll feel better soon."

"Are we done?"

"No. I have a 'toy' to show you. There've been improvements to the TPM since you used it last."

The doctor glanced at Felix from behind a desk. Its surface was empty but for a small hologram. They were seated in a cubicle that served as an office and consulting room. They'd just come from a treatment station where Felix had received various chemical "boosters." He was rubbing his arm where a welt had formed.

"What sort of improvements?" Felix asked.

"Here," the doctor answered, taking a bundle out. Removing a cloth, he disclosed a figurine. It was three inches high and resembled a woman in Roman garb. She carried a horn full of fruit and was wearing a crown.

"It's beautiful," Felix said, inspecting it closely. "It must be Fortuna."

"It is. It can't hurt to have this goddess on your side. But this figurine has a different use. Touch it and you'll see what I mean."

"It feels odd," Felix said, stroking it gently, "as if it were electrified."

"That's right," the doctor said. "Last year we set up portals in a host of ancient temples. This is what your father made me do for him. And by programming that 'child' with four different dates, I enabled him to jump from one time to the next, once he steps into a temple's precinct. I should have let your father shoot me. If his plan succeeds and the plague returns …"

The doctor's lips were trembling and he was unable to finish. Felix could hardly believe his emotion, and this despite his ERR. At the same time he had to get him back on course. "You were discussing this figurine," he prompted.

"I'm sorry," the doctor apologized. "Essentially it's a portal you can carry on your person."

"Are you serious?" Felix asked. He looked at the statue dubiously. It had an electric feel, but seemed normal enough.

"It's programmed with the same dates as the 'child's,'" Dr. Lee explained. "71 BCE, 2111, and 48 BCE — the fourth date hasn't been decoded yet. You choose a date by twisting the head to one of three slots. But there's more. To move forward in time, you must raise the right arm. To move backward, raise the left. These determine the flow of the charge. Is that clear?"

Felix nodded appreciatively and smiled at the doctor. Dr. Lee tried to smile, but wasn't up to the task. Instead his eyes drifted to the hologram beside him. As hard as he tried not to, Felix eyed the picture, too.

It was a portrait of the doctor's son and showed the date of his demise: June 7, 2213. Hating to intrude on the doctor's grief, Felix turned his eyes away, even though the picture seemed to plead for attention.

"A couple more things," the doctor went on, looking up from the portrait, "the figurine is charged to carry two people. There are no mass restrictions this time around. And unlike the charge in the various temples, no DNA protocols are in effect."

"So anyone could use this figurine?" Felix asked.

"Yes. That 'child' must be stopped. Killing him could prove messy. The alternative is to carry him here and that explains the double charge. You only have to touch him while your portal is engaged and both of you will jump to the future."

"Good," Felix said. He was glad to hear no killing would be necessary. Just the thought of stabbing someone turned his stomach. "You said a couple of things. There's something else?"

"Yes. But it's good news. The 'child's' charge is limited."

"Limited? What does that mean?"

"He can last three weeks in each place, maximum. After that, the portal's charge will die. We'll dispatch you to your entry point of old — Panarium, 71 BCE. If you do exactly what you did last time, you'll meet up with Aceticus. Once you do, you'll protect him for a week. After that, the 'child' will be gone."

"You mean, he'll be forced to jump to his second destination?"

"Yes. The tracer in his blood will move him along. Unless you bring him here, that is."

"Okay," Felix said. The task seemed difficult, but there was no point complaining. It had to be done and that was that.

"Well then," the doctor said, "it only remains to wish you luck."

"Thank you," Felix said, climbing to his feet.

"And Felix?" the doctor said, as Felix reached the exit.

"Yes?"

"My son's name was Charlie. He was a good boy and you would have liked him."

"I'm very sorry, Dr. Lee."

"I'm sorry too. More than I can say."

"You have your toga *virilis*. Its fibres are dense and will serve as body armour. They're also waterproof and lice-resistant. Like last time, you'll be wearing modern underwear. And you have a pouch with cinnamon, a pinch of which is worth a fortune."

Professor MacPherson gave Felix a sidelong glance and his glasses reflected the light from the ceiling. Felix almost chuckled. Even his dad avoided glasses and had accepted vision implants. It was odd to see someone with glasses on his nose, as if he'd just stepped forth from a history textbook. But there was no denying the vigour in his stare. Like Felix and his father, the professor had avoided ERR and confronted the world with his feelings intact. Unfortunately these had aged him quickly. His wrinkles had multiplied since last year, and he appeared much frailer, more prune-like, too. He also seemed more kindly, if that was possible. He addressed Felix as *fili mi*, the way his father had.

His father. Felix had asked to see him, if only for a minute. The general had been reluctant. Mr. Taylor was in bad condition: the shock from the stun-rod had affected him badly and he still hadn't recovered fully. When Felix had insisted, the general had shrugged and addressed Bernard, the Station's operating system. An image of his dad had appeared on a screen. He was lying on a pallet and staring at the ceiling. He'd seemed to be in a trance of sorts. Unable to endure this sight, Felix had nodded and the screen had gone blank.

"What about your identity?" the professor continued, closing a cabinet door that kept swivelling open. This cabinet was old and crammed full of books and other objects. These contents kept causing its door to open and every few minutes the professor would slam it closed.

"The old one won't do," Felix said, smiling at the professor's irritation. It had been a long time since he'd seen such emotion. "Even though my entry point will be the same."

"The same?" the professor asked, staring at Felix. "I believe we sent you to Panarium last year. On June 15, 71 BCE."

"You did," Felix agreed.

"Yet this 'child' jumped to Cremona, on May 30?"

"That's right. He's after Aceticus and hopes to find him in Cremona."

"So shouldn't you follow him and proceed to May instead of June?"

"Aceticus wasn't in Cremona. He was visiting Rome."

"What?" the professor asked, with a look of surprise. Again, Felix wanted to laugh. Displays of emotion were so uncommon that a look of surprise resembled full-out shock.

"I never told you. I met Aceticus on my trip last year."

"You met Aceticus?"

"Yes, at the Circus Maximus. He'd been in Rome awhile. If my entry point is the same as last time, I'll be sure to see him before that 'child' does. That's why my old identity won't work. Last time I was Aceticus' adopted son."

"I see," the professor mused. Because of his glasses, his eyes looked more turtle-like than human. The cabinet door opened and struck his head. With a mild curse, he slammed it closed. Again Felix had to suppress a chuckle.

"All right," MacPherson said. "I have it. We'll make you someone of Celtic descent — this is true of many citizens in Cisalpine Gaul. This will explain your complexion and green-blue eyes. You're travelling to Rome on family business. But where do you live and what's your name?"

"I'm from Mantua," Felix said without hesitation, "and my name is Marcus Vergilius Maro, although my friends call me Felix."

"A clever choice," the professor laughed. "Mantua is in Cisalpine Gaul and the Vergilii clan hail from this town. Well that's everything, except …"

"Except?"

"Two things. First, you must be careful. The Romans aren't like us, you know. They are passionate, strong, and very physical. Magnificent creatures, but easily insulted. Don't let your guard down for a moment, *puer*."

"That's one thing. Is there something else?"

"Yes," the professor said, removing his glasses. "I don't believe your father's guilty. A learned man like him could never be so barbaric. Just so you know."

"Thank you, Professor. Your words mean a lot." He didn't mention what he thought of his dad: that he was bitter, guilty, and utterly despicable. Instead he took his toga and left the office. The old man was watching him like a kindly hawk and didn't even notice when, for the twentieth time, the cabinet door opened. As if directed by a ghostly hand, it banged him on the back of his skull.

Felix was walking to his quarters. The TPM was charging still and scheduled to be ready in roughly three hours. In the meantime he would rest, if his worries allowed him to.

"Felix!"

Would he survive the trip? The last time round, he'd almost died. Only luck and Carolyn had kept him alive. But Carolyn wasn't coming and his luck could fail him.

"Felix! Wait up!"

More disturbing was the subject of his father. What did all his learning come to? What difference did it make that he collected books and worked to preserve the historical record if he was plotting to kill every human on Earth? So people ignored the past. So the Repository might be shuttered. As terrible as this was, it didn't give him the right …

"Felix! Stop!"

He turned on his heel and his mouth dropped open. Carolyn stood behind him. She was in a Klytex gown that reached down to her ankles and was wearing a pair of three-inch heels. Her hair was in a bun and her skin was tinted — she'd changed her colouring to please Stephen Gowan. Despite his tension, he managed to laugh.

"You're all dressed up for Halo Ball, I see."

"This is no time for jokes! My dad told me the news and I rushed back to see you. You can't go. You know that, don't you?"

"What's the alternative? We let Aceticus die?"

"You can't be sure that's the plan! After all, you know your father. Even if he used the TPM, there's no way he'd try to resurrect the plague!"

"I thought I knew my father," Felix said sadly, "but the facts are clear. That 'child' is tracking Aceticus. If he succeeds, well, you've seen the results."

He was referring to the fact that, the year before, they'd returned to a world that had been empty of humans.

"You can't go back!" she insisted. "Those Romans are crazy! If they don't stab you or beat you to death, they'll find a hundred other ways to kill you! Stay with us and take your chances!"

Her eyes met his. They were cold as ice and well-controlled. When Felix smiled, she couldn't smile back.

"I appreciate your concern," he said, "but I have no choice. I should also get some rest because I'll be leaving in three hours."

He smiled, turned, and walked away. He hadn't taken three steps when an object struck his head. Wheeling about, he saw that Carolyn had tossed a shoe at him. He was going to speak when she tossed the other shoe as well. If he hadn't ducked, it would have struck his face. Without a word, she walked off and vanished around a bend.

Her message was clear. She was washing her hands of this stupid affair.

Three hours and nineteen minutes later, Felix was on the threshold of a transparent sphere. It was twelve feet tall and its membrane was golden. Its interior was filled with multiple gases that were swirling and contained every shade of the rainbow. Surrounding Felix was a mass of equipment, processors, signallers, high-energy conductors. The temperature was elevated, but he had to focus hard to keep himself from trembling.

"You have everything?" the general asked.

"Yes."

"You won't change your mind?"

"Only if you have a better idea."

"I don't," he admitted. "If your dad's out to get us, you're our only solution. And I misjudged you, Felix. I assumed the apple doesn't fall far from the tree. I was wrong. Dead wrong. No hard feelings, I hope."

"None whatsoever. Let's get this show on the road."

General Manes nodded and the pair shook hands. Felix turned and faced the sphere, his muscles tensing up. The doctor was at a console over on a catwalk. When Felix signalled him, the countdown would start and …

Wait. There was someone beside him. Not someone but … Carolyn. Like Felix, she was dressed in Roman garb. He was going to speak, but she shook her head decisively.

When he nodded to the doctor and the countdown began, his hand was steadier than it had been all afternoon.

Chapter Seven

The *hoplomachus* tried to strike the *murmillo*. The older gladiator blocked the thrust, but slipped and struggled to regain his balance. Thirty thousand voices screamed, producing a roar that almost burst Felix's eardrums. He also thought his nose would melt. Many spectators hadn't bathed in a while and the stink was awful. To distract himself from the mind-numbing stench, he gazed across the space before him, past its central *spina* of statues and pillars, its starting gates for chariot races, and its tiers that could hold two hundred thousand people. *Not too shabby*, he thought.

The last day had been peculiar. First, there'd been the projection itself. Hurtling through the cracks of the cosmos, he'd felt a billion unseen hands yank his particles down a path of radiation. His limbs had been stretched over a thousand light years and he'd witnessed the birth and death of galaxies, all within a heartbeat. Then everything had snapped together and he'd wound up, with Carolyn, in the *cella* of Minerva's temple.

From the temple they'd journeyed to Panarium, a small town on the outskirts of Rome. Tracking down the vendor they'd met the last time round, Felix had purchased two pieces of pastry, paying with cinnamon from a hidden pouch. As expected, some soldiers had spied the spice and done their best to take it away. He and Carolyn had fought them off until General Pompey had intervened. Hearing that Felix knew Aceticus by reputation, he'd invited them to come to Rome, just as he'd done the last time around. They'd attended a feast where, among other things, Felix had quoted a few lines from Virgil (whose *Aeneid* hadn't yet been written) and so impressed Pompey that the general had invited him to attend this *munus*. That's why he was watching these men fight to the finish, fully aware the *murmillo* would win. As awful as this contest was, Aceticus was scheduled to appear when it ended.

"It's like I said last time," Carolyn said, eyeing the contestants, "the older man's the better fighter."

"What did she say?" a thickset man of middling height demanded. His face was wide and very good-natured, but his eyes contained an unpredictable fire. This was Gnaius Pompey Magnus.

"She said the *murmillo* is stronger," Felix answered. To explain Carolyn's awful Latin, he'd said she was visiting from Aquitania, a part of Gaul untouched by Rome. He explained that her father had died three months back and Carolyn had been forced to move in with his family.

"My thoughts exactly," Pompey replied. He turned to the large man sitting on his right, a swarthy fellow with sagging jowls that gave him a comic, hang-dog expression. This was Marcus Licinius Crassus, a Roman general and the city's richest citizen. He'd been hanging about since the evening before. "Crassus, twelve *aurei* say that the *murmillo* beats the *hoplomachus*. Do you accept the bet?"

"It amazes me, Magnus, how you never learn your lesson and unfailingly back the weaker party. I stake twelve *aurei* on the *hoplomachus*."

Felix shook his head in disbelief. It was strange to know what was going to happen, what people would say, who would hurt whom, as if the entire population, a swarm of people, were actors in a drama and had memorized their lines.

But it was creepy knowing how this match would end. The *hoplomachus* had grazed his rival's forearm and was stabbing left and right with his eight-foot spear. Felix glanced at a woman nearby. *She'll shout "skewer him, stab him like a chicken,"* he thought. Sure enough, she suddenly yelled, "Skewer him! Stab him like a chicken!"

Felix smiled grimly.

"When will this end?" Carolyn said through gritted teeth.

"We're almost there," Felix assured her, as the *murmillo* lashed out suddenly and knocked his rival flat. The crowd started shouting, "Celadus! Celadus!" as did the woman who, just seconds before, had wanted to see Celadus stabbed like a chicken.

On cue, the audience turned to Pompey. It was his right to decide the warrior's fate. As before, he invited Carolyn to judge. Her preference was to save the *hoplomachus*, but this might have caused a butterfly effect. For a second time she refused this honour and so condemned the man to death. Pompey brought his thumb down and Celadus stabbed his rival. As Felix and Carolyn shuddered in horror, someone hailed them from behind. Felix turned and sighed with relief. The orator Cicero drew near with an old man in tow whose face was familiar: the historian Aceticus. How lucky that the "child" hadn't got to him yet.

"It gets interesting now," Felix whispered. "We no longer know how events will unfold."

"I hope there's no repeat of last year's drama," she said. She was referring to the fact that Felix had been stabbed at this juncture.

"There won't be," he promised. "I haven't said I'm Aceticus' son; just that I know of him by word of mouth. No one will think we're up to no good."

By now Aceticus had joined the group. While the historian was Pompey's client, the general was inclined to treat him as an equal, describing him to Crassus as an old family friend. He motioned Felix forward and introduced the pair.

"Where are you from?" Aceticus asked, with a kindly smile. He didn't notice Carolyn; as a female and non-citizen, she didn't count.

"From Andes, outside Mantua, *domine*."

"I've heard Mantua is beautiful," Aceticus went on, "but have never seen it."

"It's off the *Via Postumia* and difficult to get to."

"According to Pompeius Magnus, you are acquainted with my name?"

"That is correct, *domine*. Rumour has it that you're writing a book."

"Indeed I am!" he cried, his wrinkled face lighting up with joy. "It is the passion of my old age and the sole reason I rise each morning. If I had no such project, I'd be utterly lost. How delightful my *Historiae* are known beyond my study, even if they're not yet complete!"

Some spectators were grumbling. A *retiarius* was fighting a *thraex*. The latter was about to move in for the kill. Pompey's group was blocking the view. Hearing the complaints, the general climbed some stairs and headed to an exit. His friends immediately followed in his wake.

The group passed beneath a series of arches. Aceticus was asking Pompey about his time in Spain — the general had just returned from the province. Cicero was discussing Spartacus with Crassus, but the billionaire was listening in on Pompey: they were competitors and Crassus wanted to hear what his rival was saying. In fact, he went one step further. Calling the group to a stop, he invited everyone to his house for dinner, Felix and Carolyn included. He also offered them an escort home, or the choice of passing the night in his *domus*; walking the city after dark was a bad idea. After a moment's hesitation, everyone accepted.

They'd passed the stadium's western exit, which led directly to the Aventine Hill. Crassus's *domus* lay on its slopes. Felix squinted in the afternoon sun. In the distance he could see the Tiber River and warehouses belonging to the *Porticus Aemilia*. The Temple of Mercury stood on his left. Carolyn had carried him here when he'd been stabbed the last time around. The memory caused his ribs to tingle. On his right was another temple, modest in size and with worn, Tuscan columns. A crowd had gathered out in front.

They were there in the thousands, pushing and straining. Off to one side was a wall of wagons, packed to the breaking point with baskets of grain. Three men were handing these baskets out, even as they enjoined the crowd to form three lines. The crowd barely listened and kept surging as close as they could to the wagons. A knot of soldiers was standing guard, but looked very uneasy.

"Is that Ceres's temple?" Aceticus asked, squinting hard to take in the scene.

"It is indeed," Cicero answered. "Believe it or not, this is a *congiarium*."

"Let's move in closer," Crassus suggested, stepping ahead of the group.

The others followed. As the historian pressed forward, Carolyn and Felix stuck to him. At the same time, Felix explained the *congiarium*. The crowd was there to get a free handout of grain, enough food to last them a week or so. This dole was a common political tool. The people who'd received this gift would support the politician who'd provided it.

"So it's a form of bribery?" Carolyn said.

"Yes."

"It's wrong to control a population this way."

"But it's not wrong to control them with ERR," Felix countered dryly.

Pompey had climbed a wall and was surveying the scene. Crassus joined him, Cicero, too. Aceticus was flitting on the edge of the crowd, not trusting his balance to stand on the wall. Eyeing him, Felix wondered how they'd guard him day and night. If the "child" was out there, he could strike at will these next six days; after that his charge would expire. The question was how could they protect the old man day and night for almost a week?

"This won't be easy," Carolyn said, reading his thoughts. "He'll ask us why we're breathing down his neck."

"I know," Felix agreed. "We'll have to think of an answer."

He turned back to Aceticus. The officials were slow in distributing the grain and the crowd was growing restless. People were booing and yelling insults. These provoked further shouts, as well as laughter and bursts of song. The lines grew less orderly and people pushed toward the wagons. The soldiers tried to force them back, but their numbers were too few. Some bystanders managed to grab a few baskets. Their triumph further enflamed the crowd who, fearing the baskets would run out soon, dropped all semblance of order and forced their way forward. The soldiers were helpless to thrust them back. With laughter, shouts, jeers, and song, the mob knocked the wagons over and made off with the grain. The situation was potentially dangerous, but Felix had to grin. Everyone was so magnificently human.

"There's emotion for you." Carolyn sniffed.

Felix nodded then turned his gaze elsewhere. Someone else was watching the crowd from the temple's raised stylobate. His tall, thin figure, senator's robe, and perfect poise commanded people's respect. He was smiling coyly, as if amused by the chaos. As the shouts got louder and the tumult increased, his hardened features broke into a grin.

"Do you know who that is?" Felix demanded, pointing the man out. Without awaiting her reply, he said, "That's Julius Caesar."

"Julius who?"

In a rush of words, Felix explained that Caesar would become the city's chief politician, that he would subdue the untamed parts of Gaul, then turn his forces on Pompey and Rome. In some ways Caesar would save the empire, but at the cost of slaughtering many people. As he spoke, he saw Pompey had noticed Caesar, too. Leaving the wall, the general sailed into the crowd and stood beside Caesar on the temple's platform. Hating to be left out, Crassus followed suit. The two were soon chatting with Caesar, who seemed happy to have the generals there.

"History's being made," Felix said. "The first triumvirate is taking shape."

Carolyn wasn't listening. With a gasp of panic she'd left his side and was racing toward Aceticus. Felix flinched then shot off, too. While he'd been busy watching Caesar, a man had zeroed in on the senior. This thug was very short and thin, much like a child. In his hand was a dagger.

Felix ran hard. He moved so fast that he and Carolyn hit the "child" at the same time, just as he was lifting his knife to strike. Felix swept his legs from under him, while Carolyn punched him twice in the chest. He dropped like a stone.

They grabbed him by his tunic. Ignoring the man's cries, Felix said in Common Speak that the game was up and they were taking him home. His fingers were closing on his statue already, to whisk the guy off before he tried to escape.

"I don't understand," he gasped in Latin. "Speak Latin, if you can. And how was I to know the geezer was your friend? I didn't mean to hurt him. I just wanted his purse."

"You're speaking Latin," Felix said, momentarily nonplussed.

"What else would I be speaking?" the man practically spat. "Some of us were born in this city. We don't use Greek or that cow speech of yours."

"You were born here...?"

"On the *Vicus Armilustri*! Listen, *domine*, I've done no harm. There's no need to get the *vigiles* involved ..."

"It's not him," Felix told Carolyn. "He's just a thief."

"So I see," Carolyn said.

"But the 'child' is here," Felix said. "Or so my instincts tell me."

"You just think that," she said wryly, "because everyone here looks capable of murder."

Chapter Eight

Alighting on a birdbath, a sparrow drank some water and shook its wings. The afternoon light played upon its plumage, it harshness filtered by a line of trees and an exuberant rhododendron bush. Water splashed onto the mosaic floor and struck a marble bust in a corner. The bust resembled Crassus closely and Felix assumed it was a portrait of some ancestor.

The scene was enchanting. They were standing in a *peristylium* whose dimensions put the Taylors' unit to shame. And it was only part of the two-storey *domus*, whose *vestibulum*, *atrium*, and other rooms were beautifully arranged. The *hortus* too was a feast for the eyes.

The sparrow was still drinking when an advancing presence caused it to take wing. Felix smiled as Carolyn drew near. They'd arrived at Crassus's home shortly before. While the other guests were resting up, Carolyn, like Felix, wished to stretch her legs. She was adjusting her *palla* as she walked up to him.

"Want help?" he asked, as she fiddled with its folds.

"That's okay. I can manage."

But she couldn't. She'd piled the material too much on one side and all of it suddenly slipped to the tiles, leaving her in nothing but a linen tunic. As she retrieved the cloak, Felix spied a scar on her shoulder. It was perfectly round and an inch in diameter. Only a precision instrument could have left such a mark.

"What's that?" he asked.

"None of your business," she snapped back. By now the *palla* was back in place and she was pinning its heavy folds together. For this, she had a wooden brooch in hand.

"I shouldn't have asked," he apologized. "This is quite some garden, isn't it?"

"It's pretty," she conceded. Aware he hadn't meant any harm, she explained, "To tell you the truth, I'm not sure what it's from. But it's no big deal."

"Okay."

She would have said more, but they were interrupted. Emerging from a doorway that led to the *cucina*, three servants in aprons led a sheep into the garden. The beast was docile and ambled to a stone block in the corner. Felix and Carolyn were thunderstruck. Such animals were rare in their own day and age.

"I've never seen a goat," she murmured. "Not even in a zoo."

"That's not a goat," Felix corrected her. "I think it's a sheep."

They watched as the servants fed the animal grain and stroked its fur affectionately. One was carrying a fair-sized basket. They were laughing and talking softly together.

"I don't know how you do it," Carolyn said. Her eyes were on the sheep still and, while her ERR wouldn't let her smile, she was feeling something close to contentment.

"Do what?"

"How you negotiate this world. It pulls in every direction at once and barely gives you space to breathe. One moment it's beautiful and people are charming; the next they're doing despicable things."

"I guess I've been taught to expect such complications. They're what make us interesting, my dad always says. Our genius to build is matched by our desire to harm."

"I guess."

The sheep bleated plaintively. The men were gripping it tightly now and holding it over the shelf of stone. The beast hated being handled so and was putting up a struggle. Its angry bleating was loud and comical. Again Carolyn almost managed a smile.

"We could have been born in this age," Felix observed, chuckling too at the sheep's pathetic kicking. "All of this might have struck us as normal."

"Normal doesn't mean admirable."

"Maybe. But you can't dismiss it casually, either. It must have value...."

As if to sabotage this statement, there was a ghastly shriek from the sheep. One servant had drawn its head back and bared its throat to the world. A second had pulled a knife from the basket and, with one deft movement, passed the blade across its jugular. There was a spurt of blood and, with the last of its breath, the sheep was making a horrific sound, high-pitched, pained and full of panic. It was attempting to breathe, but the air wouldn't come. It was kicking out spasmodically but the men held on tight. And there was no escaping the iron grip of death.

One of them caught sight of the pair. With blood from the sheep trickling from his chin, he cried, "You two will be feasting this evening!"

"I don't care what you say." Carolyn sniffed, her ERR barely hiding her scorn. "These people are barbaric. As soon as we've escaped this place, I'm going to delete these terrible memories forever."

She stalked off. Felix was thinking along the same lines when he saw a servant lean toward the beast, whisper to it, and scratch its ears. It was like watching someone bid a friend farewell.

He shook his head. They were so rough and yet so tender, these puzzling people.

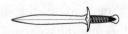

"You can't fight slaves on an empty belly, Magnus! Have more sheep! It's fresh off the grill!"

"I can't chase Spartacus if I'm stuffed like Maccus in the *fabula Atellanae!* It's Caesar who should eat more! He's thin as a rake!"

"If I eat any more, I'll turn into a sheep and become another face in the crowd!"

"But at least you'll grow your hair back, Caesar! Instead of those strands, you'll have a rug of wool!"

Felix was watching the proceedings with interest. They were in the *triclinium* with the other guests, Aceticus, Cicero, and Julius Caesar. The room was spacious, although the ceiling was low. Its mosaic floor displayed a complex design, at the heart of which was Bacchus, the merry god of wine. The walls were panelled and showed scenes of famous myths: Romulus slaying his brother Remus, the Horatii and Curiatii, and Dido cursing Aeneas.

The room's arrangement came as no surprise as he'd attended such a feast just the night before. The dining room held three long couches, forming a square with one side missing. Three tables sat in the middle of this space, each laden with platters of food. Crassus was on the head couch, reclining in the middle, with Caesar to his left and Pompey to his right. Aceticus and Cicero were lying across from Felix. Along with Carolyn, he occupied the leftmost *lectus*.

"Speaking of Spartacus," Pompey drawled, "will you be attending me, Aceticus?"

"Of course, *domine*," the historian answered. "I'd be honoured to follow."

"What business does an old man have with war?" Crassus asked.

"He wishes to see the campaign," Pompey explained, "so that he can describe it in his upcoming book."

"I wonder if he'll mention me," Crassus growled. "It's funny how I'm the commander-in-chief, yet no one notices my *imperium*...."

Crassus's remark triggered a discussion with Pompey. As the other guests listened — Caesar seemed amused — Felix addressed Carolyn. She was looking at her plate and was famished still. She'd eaten a few oysters and a boiled egg, but had ignored the sheep, for obvious reasons.

"Aceticus will be marching with Pompey," he whispered.

"That's good news," she answered dully. "If Pompey lets us tag along, guarding Aceticus should be easy."

"That's what I'm thinking. Look," he insisted, "you have to eat. Starving yourself won't bring the sheep back to life."

"I can't believe they'd kill an animal like that."

"We would too if we didn't clone our food."

"We don't clone humans. That doesn't mean we slaughter them."

"You know what I'm saying. They kill these animals because they have to eat. And you do, too. You can't guard Aceticus on an empty stomach."

When Carolyn nodded grudgingly, Felix asked a slave if he could serve her some meat. She bit into it moments later and admitted it was tasty.

By now the conversation had changed direction.

"So Caesar," Crassus asked, setting down his wine, "are you pleased with the *congiarium?*"

"Very," he answered. "It went well." His voice was deep and beautifully pitched. He was just another guest in the room, but it was impossible for the others to take their eyes off him.

"It's a form of bribery and upsets our traditions," Cicero protested. "These *plebs* will vote for you in the next elections, but only because you've given them free grain."

"They will vote for me," Caesar corrected him, "because I appeal to their reason and not their sentiment. Instead of begging them to keep our ways alive, I ask them to consider where their own profit lies. By approaching them in this logical vein, I'll make them the equal of their so-called betters."

"Be careful Caesar," Cicero countered. "A state that's 'reasonable' and rejects its past will alter itself beyond all recognition. Who can say what sort of change you'll usher in and whether it will work to people's profit or pain? The past binds citizens together, like mortar binding bricks to form a house. If you dispense with it too breezily, people will see no reason to behave as one."

"The present owes nothing to the past," Caesar said with a dismissive shrug. "And you're not worried about our traditions as much as the change of status that you might suffer. Have no fear, Cicero. By appealing to the *plebs'* good sense, the worst I can do is turn them into *nobiles* like you."

"If I knew that was the worst you could do,

I wouldn't complain. But what if the *plebs*, drunk on reason, throw our mores out and make *us* like them? Reason is a threshing blade. By all means it harvests the autumn crop, but it trims every stalk to an identical height and allows no excellence to thrive whatsoever."

"Equality is the future," Caesar said with a laugh.

"And if this equality eradicates our virtue?" Cicero cried.

"Virtue is just an excuse for sticking with the past. The real values we're pursuing are comfort and equality."

"Virtue is independent of comfort," Cicero exclaimed. "It shines forth in times of need or plenty, war or peace, labour or leisure. The starving man needs no food to gain virtue, nor the poor man money, nor the sick man health. By championing reason, equality and comfort, and expecting no show of virtue in return, you treat our people as if they were swine and cattle."

"Perhaps that's so," Caesar conceded, "but it is the future, whether you like or not."

As the others spoke in turn, Felix mulled over this exchange. His own world was a product of Caesar's views, one in which comfort and equality thrived, but in which virtue was practically non-existent. Three days ago he would have quarrelled with Caesar and agreed with Cicero. Now that the world was under threat and the plague was rearing its head again, he was thinking Caesar might be right and comfort was more desirable than virtue. Unless …

He flinched. Caesar was eyeing him and he had to focus.

"Gentlemen, we've ignored our foreign guests. I gather, *adolescens*, you are of Gallic descent and a very fine poet. And your cousin is from Aquitania. This is a rare opportunity and I'd like to profit from your knowledge. Tell me. What is Gaul like, the parts we Romans haven't conquered yet?"

Caesar winked at the room, as if to say, "Let's have some fun." His smile quickly vanished, however, when Felix cleared his throat and addressed his question squarely. If he impressed the group, he told himself, Pompey might let them follow his army and enable them to watch Aceticus closely. At the same time he could have some fun of his own.

"I'm glad to answer your questions, Gaius Julius Caesar," he replied. "*Gallia est omnis divisa in partes tres, quarum unam incolunt Belgae, aliam Aquitani, tertiam qui ipsorum lingua Celtae, nostra Galli appellantur. Hi omnes lingua, institutis, legibus inter se differunt....*"

He would later translate for Carolyn: "All of Gaul is divided into three parts. The Belgae live in one of these, the Aquitani in a second, while the third is inhabited by the Galli, who call themselves Celts in their native language. These three peoples differ from each other in their language, laws, and institutions...."

Like the night before, the guests let out a gasp. All loved to hear first-rate Latin recited, and this little speech was immensely polished. The group applauded loudly and shook their heads in admiration.

"Last night you feasted us on poetry," Crassus said, "and tonight you have graced us with this beautiful prose. I can't thank you enough. You have stirred my spirit."

"*Adolescens*," Cicero added, "my own Latin is inferior to none, but clearly your gift is equal to mine. What joy to hear such balance and precision! Surely such speech is food for the gods!"

"I could polish my history for fifty years, and still not achieve your ease of expression," Aceticus wailed. His tone was heavy and pregnant with envy.

"For delighting us," Pompey said, "ask any favour and I shall grant it on the spot."

Caesar was the last to speak. "I swear, *adolescens*, if I were to write a book, this would be my style. My head buzzes because your speech is so close to my own."

These compliments paid, the men turned to other subjects. Crassus mentioned a plague in the south, and the others discussed this frightening outbreak. Felix turned to Carolyn, grinning widely.

"You look pleased," she said.

"I am," he answered. "I just quoted from a book that Caesar will write one day. No wonder he enjoyed my speech so much."

He explained that Pompey had also promised him a favour. This meant they'd be able to escort his troops and guard Aceticus against assassination. Everything was working out better than he'd hoped.

"Maybe so," Carolyn said, "but you're taking risks. By quoting from these future works, you just might trigger a butterfly effect. If I were you, I'd be more careful."

Instead of answering, Felix asked if she was finished with her meat. When she said no, he took some from her plate. The meat was fatty, rich, and delicious. He was thinking he'd never felt so accomplished before, so thrilled, so elated, so appreciated ... when a crunch rang out and he grimaced in pain.

He'd bitten down on a piece of bone.

Chapter Nine

"We'll meet back here in an hour," Pompey said, his eyes still bleary from last night's drinking. "Don't be late because I'm leaving once my bath is done."

As a chorus of voices promised to be punctual, Pompey led Caesar into the *Balineum Fausti*. After a moment's hesitation, Aceticus followed.

Before retiring the previous night, Felix had asked Pompey if he and his "cousin" could join his troops. Still delighted with Felix's speech, Pompey had agreed. Shortly before sunrise his slave had roused them and they'd swallowed down some bread and milk. They'd then followed Pompey to the Campus Martius, along with Caesar and the old historian. As they'd passed the *Balineum Fausti*, Pompey had decided he needed to bathe and invited the rest of the group to join him.

"It doesn't look hygienic," Carolyn told Felix, surveying a lofty entrance that was set with arches in which pigeons were roosting. The mosaic floor was cracked and faded, garbage was piled in the courtyard's corners, and the walls' red brick was pitted with age. An unshaven janitor was scratching at his armpits. It was likely he had body lice.

"The Romans are known for their cleanliness," Felix replied. "There are hundreds of baths like this in the city."

"That explains why the crowds smell so fresh," she said acidly. "Still, we haven't much choice. You'll keep an eye on you know who?" She gestured to Aceticus.

"Of course."

"I'm not a good judge of such things, but he seems less cheerful."

"It's funny you say that. I was thinking he seemed down, as well."

"Well, see you later. And don't forget to wash behind your ears."

Making a face, Felix entered the men's section. Navigating a corridor and brushing past a curtain, he came upon the *apodyteria*. Here he handed his clothes to Pompey's slave, Flaccus, who folded them neatly and placed them on a shelf. Promising to keep an eye on his belongings, he handed Felix a pair of clogs to protect his feet from the heated tiling underfoot.

Felix entered the *tepidarium*, a square hall built of marble and stucco. It was twenty metres long and topped with a dome. The latter was built of travertine marble that was painted with a charming scene of

the gods staring down from Mount Olympus. In
addition to the handsome decor, the room was toasty
warm. The floor was sitting on stacks of tiles (these
were known as as *hypocausts*). They absorbed and
spread the heat from a furnace. The more "stacks"
there were, the hotter the room was.

The hall contained a line of tables. Two strangers
were lying on a pair of them and slaves were busy
massaging their muscles. Groaning as their limbs
were pounded, these men talked shop. One was a
sausage-seller and complaining how the plague was
cutting into his business. Aceticus wasn't present so
Felix passed on.

Slipping past a curtain, he entered the *caldarium*.
This space was hotter than the previous one and
filled with billowing steam. It contained a pool
in which a man sat, singing to the room. Moving
forward gingerly, Felix almost knocked into a
statue. There. Aceticus was in an alcove, the so-
called *laconicum* or hottest part of the bath. He
was stark naked, seated on a marble slab and easy
pickings for any would-be assassin. Oblivious to
his danger, he was rubbing oil into his skin. Again,
Felix thought his spirits seemed down.

"You've been abandoned, *magister*?" Felix asked.

"Caesar and Pompey require privacy." The old
man sighed. "They're in the *palaestra*, which is
empty now. So yes, they have abandoned me. But
sit, *puer*. Unless you wish to leave me, too?"

Expressing thanks, Felix sat on the slab and
winced at the touch of the heated stone. He was

sweating heavily because of the steam. The man in the pool was singing louder now and his deep voice echoed round the chamber.

"It should be interesting to see Pompey's troops," Felix said, as he reached for the oil and applied it to his skin. It was pleasant to the touch.

"It is a task I will forego," Aceticus said tersely. "Once we've finished here, I intend to go home."

"Oh?" Felix gasped, with a note of worry. If the historian went home, how would they protect him? "Are you not feeling up to the trip, *magister*?"

"It's not my health that concerns me," the old man said, "so much as my talent."

"I don't understand...."

"A man like you wouldn't!" Aceticus cried. His tone was openly bitter now. "When I conceived my *Historiae* years ago, my intention was to rival Herodotus himself. My learning and insight would have been prodigious, and my language would have cut like tempered steel."

He paused and took a *strigil* in hand, a curved metal blade, about six inches long. Passing this along his arm, he removed the oil he'd applied minutes earlier.

"After hearing your address last night," he said, flicking the spent oil into a pail, "I realized how sterile my efforts are. You captured your subject with the force of a soldier, while my *Historiae* are the work of a man who's never left his study for the world at large. Until yesterday my writing was a refuge from old age; after hearing you I understand my skills are non-existent."

"You exaggerate your failings, *domine*," Felix observed, struggling hard to keep his limbs from trembling. Surely Aceticus wasn't saying…?

"If anything, I'm being kind to myself." He had scraped the other arm free of oil and was working on his legs. "Our city is the wonder of the world. Word of our feats will dazzle future generations. Such tales require a brilliant handling and, as your speech taught me yesterday, I lack such talent. It pains me to say so, but I cannot join Pompey and chronicle his feats. His genius deserves better than my mediocrity. So I'll return to Cremona and burn the pages I've written. That done, I shall speedily take leave of this world."

"You can't!" Felix cried. "You have to continue! Your book will be inspiring, I promise!" His voice was so loud that it echoed round the chamber. The man in the pool stopped singing a moment, puzzled by this outburst. Seconds later, he resumed.

"No, *adolescens*," the historian said with a chuckle, flicking more oil into the pail. "If I don't want critics to laugh at my style, silence is my best defence." He stood and set the *strigil* down. "I will dress and bid Pompey farewell. If he needs someone to describe his feats, he can always turn to you."

That said, he strode off into the billowing steam. The tapping from his clogs grew steadily fainter as he returned to the *tepidarium* and proceeded to the changing rooms. Felix felt like vomiting. He'd spoiled everything! Embittered because of last night's recital, Aceticus wouldn't write his book. That meant

Felix wouldn't read it and the plague would triumph. Because he'd yearned to show how clever he was, he'd condemned the entire planet to extinction. In fact, he'd done the assassin's job for him.

He had to change the old man's mind! How, he didn't know, but it had to be done. Grabbing the *strigil*, he scraped the oil off. He then shot into the steam and left the *caldarium* behind, along with the man's loud singing. In the *tepidarium* he almost slipped in a puddle and had to slow down. Some bathers were leaving the *apodyteria* and good manners required him to let them pass. When he entered the changing room, Aceticus was gone.

"The historian," he asked Flaccus, as he pulled his clothes on, "did he come this way?"

"He most certainly did." Flaccus yawned. "But be careful, *puer*. His mood is sour and he's inclined to bite."

Felix nodded as he draped his toga across shoulders. Rushing to the exit, he knocked into the janitor who was wiping a counter with an evil-looking rag.

"Go easy, *adolescens*," the fat man said. "Our legions can beat Spartacus without your help."

Ignoring the man, who screamed with laughter at his joke, Felix ran into the spacious courtyard. There. Aceticus was at its far end with his hands clasped behind him. He looked broken-hearted and Felix racked his brain for something cheerful to say. He barely noticed a figure who was stealing forward. This person was a bit shorter than Felix and dressed in a cloak too large for his limbs. He was also wearing an oversized hood that kept his features hidden.

"Felix!" Carolyn called. Turning around, Felix spied her. She was exiting the baths and arranging the folds of her *palla*. She lifted her gaze and saw that Felix was watching. She nodded in greeting then froze in her tracks. An instant later she was racing toward him. With a frown of confusion, Felix spun about. Now he was sprinting forward, as well.

The hooded guy was rushing the old man. He was two metres off and closing in quickly. In his right hand he was clutching a dagger. There was no mistaking his violent intentions. Aceticus had seen him, too; his sad frown had changed to a look of horror.

It was like a dream in which Felix was being chased and, as hard as he tried, there was no escape. His legs were weighted down and the air seemed to grip him, as if it contained a million microscopic hooks. Carolyn was beside him and lagging just as noticeably. Both saw the "child" grab hold of his victim and, with two, sharp movements, thrust his arms aside. Both screamed in warning as Aceticus flinched. Both saw the fall of the knife, its point aimed straight at the old man's sternum. Both howled in anguish although their screams were silent.

The world was suddenly an explosion of red.

The dagger hit the old man's diaphragm, causing him to stagger back. The assassin twisted and lunged again. This time he struck Aceticus' flank and sliced it open a good four inches. He was preparing for a third blow to the throat but Carolyn was able to block the thrust, even as Felix kicked him in the ribs. The "child" went flying.

An instant later he was on his feet. Despite his size he was remarkably strong. Punching out, he caught Carolyn on her cheek. At the same time he was able to knock Felix off balance before lunging at Aceticus to finish the job. Felix just managed to catch his ankle and trip him up. Carolyn had recovered and threw three punches. One half-winded him. With a curse he retreated and mounted a wall. Jumping from its heights, he disappeared.

Carolyn started in pursuit, but Felix stopped her.

"Let him go!" he cried. "I need help over here."

He was kneeling at the old man's side. Aceticus presented an awful sight. His white toga had two red stains that were quickly converging. His limbs trembled and his eyes were wide with shock. Felix slipped his own toga off, bunched it together, and cushioned his head. Carolyn took a place beside him. She had some medical training and was cutting the old man's toga with the "child's" blade. When the wounds were exposed, she considered them closely.

"How bad?" Felix asked.

"He struck an artery, the mesenteric," she said, probing with her fingers. "He also nicked two organs, the liver for sure and a kidney maybe. He's bleeding internally and needs lots of repairs. If we don't act, he'll die for sure."

"Can you save him?"

"Here? No way! They don't have the equipment.

And there are no antibiotics so he would die of infection. What do we do?"

Felix was thinking hard. If they couldn't fix him here, they had to take him somewhere else. The choice was obvious: the distant future.

"You can't," Carolyn said, divining his thoughts. She'd tied three tourniquets to slow the bleeding. "If you take him from this time frame, he won't have written his book. The plague will be raging and our world will die."

"I know," Felix cried. "But if we don't save him …"

A crowd had gathered. People were chattering and offering advice. Some were saying they should give the old man water, others that they should keep him warm, and others that the gods should be duly petitioned. One man observed that he'd seen worse in battle. By now Caesar and Pompey were present and looking on in horror.

"Aceticus!" Pompey called.

"Pompeius Magnus," the old man groaned. "Do not grieve. I welcome death."

"Don't talk that way!" Pompey cried. "There's life in you yet!"

"It is better so," Aceticus moaned. "A life without purpose is no life at all. I'm relieved to cross the bridge to Hades."

His words struck a chord with Felix. A bridge to Hades. A bridge. That's what Felix needed, a bridge to the future. Of course! He fumbled in his toga and brought his figurine out.

"Carolyn! I need your portal quickly!" He twisted the head on his statuette right.

"What for? I'm telling you now, you can't take him back...."

"I can maybe make a wormhole," Felix said. "No, don't say anything. Just twist your figure's head to 71 BCE. And raise its left arm to create a backward charge. I'll twist my statue to our present and make a forward charge. The two combined might form a wormhole — if Clavius was right. If so, I can take Aceticus back and freeze the effects of anything here."

"Are you sure?" she asked, taking her statue from her *palla*. She sounded doubtful.

"No. But it's worth a try. Go on. Turn the head."

As they fumbled with their portals, the bystanders thought they were praying to Fortuna. Some fell to their knees and started praying, as well. Pompey joined them. For his part, Caesar was eyeing Carolyn's shoulder and was clearly taken with her circular scar.

"I'm ready," Carolyn said.

"Okay. Now listen. If Aceticus recovers, I'm not coming back. I'll travel to the next date, 2111. Can you make your way there?"

"Yes! But you've got to move! Aceticus is slipping...!"

It was true. The historian had lost such a quantity of blood that he was shaking violently and his skin was blue. The fading light of his eyes showed that he had mere minutes to live; if he was lucky. Amazingly, he was trying to speak. Felix leaned in closer to listen.

"There's nothing left," the old man murmured. "Let me die and be forgotten."

"It isn't that easy," Felix answered. That said, he waved to Carolyn and pressed the statue's base. His eyes were closed and he expected the unusual to happen.

He wasn't disappointed.

Chapter Ten

In the car museum that Felix toured as a child, there'd been an ancient escalator that would take him from one floor to the next. He would stand on a step and the whole staircase would rise, allowing him to survey the main floor at his leisure. Although Dispersion Portals were more efficient, Felix had loved the "disappearing" staircase.

Caught in that wormhole with Aceticus beside him, he thought of the escalator as they jumped to the future. A revolving tube of light engulfed them, its rays looping back on themselves, vanishing and returning, like the escalator's steps. And just as the escalator provided a view of the museum, this "tube" gave him a view of time's permutations.

Behind him were the baths and the crowd, frozen in the instant at which he'd leaped into the future. While they grew smaller as he barrelled down the tube, their outlines remained as starkly defined. Before him were the Station and TPM, mere points in the distance, but also perfectly drawn. And in between? Countless forms stood on exhibit, like prehistoric flies paralyzed in amber. These would remain if Aceticus lived; they would melt and regroup if he died of his wounds. Felix's head was spinning. Arrayed before him was one chain of causality, with souls laid out in one version of the past. Buried in the unformed folds of the kosmos were the many other pasts that might possibly result, if any one element were drastically altered. Immensity wasn't the word for this display. He was gazing at the front door to the mansion of eternity.

Then the "tube" disgorged them.

They were positioned in the TPM. Coloured gases swirled about them and, through the sphere's transparent membrane, Felix saw the control room. With a shaky hand, he set the figurine down: so long as its charge remained stable, the wormhole would stay open. He wanted to examine its hollows, but a groan drew him back. Aceticus. His heart was on the brink of stopping.

"This man is dying!" he cried. "We need emergency treatment!"

His shouts were uncalled for. As soon as Aceticus had entered the sphere, a sensor had swiftly scanned his condition. Felix had barely spoken when three Health Drones burst in and swarmed the old man. One thrust a tube into his lungs: it would spare him from having to breathe on his own. Another sprayed his wounds with proteins, creating a "bandage" until the cuts could be sealed. The third pierced his veins and pumped in plasma, to replenish all the blood that he'd lost. At the same time the drones extended their bases, creating a stretcher on which they placed their patient. They transported him to OR 3.

"Wait," Felix cried. "Give him a Mem-gauge."

The words were barely out of his mouth when a cortical "cap" appeared on the old man's skull. It would track every memory that he formed in the Station. Once he was fit enough to go back home — assuming he survived this ordeal — they could deprive him of everything that he'd seen of the future.

Once the drones were gone, Felix sighed with relief — way too soon. In the control room he glimpsed something that was far from reassuring.

The general and Dr. Lee were standing by a console. But something was off. They were wobbling slightly, their hands were shaking, and their hair was standing on end, as if they'd both been given electrical shocks. Felix swiftly joined them.

"Felix. What's happening?" the general asked. He spoke slowly and with effort. His eyeballs, too, were shaking in their sockets.

"Aceticus was stabbed so I brought him here. I did so by creating a mini-wormhole."

"I see," the general observed without pressing for details. "Where's Carolyn?"

"She's chasing the assassin to 2111. What's wrong, sir? You don't look well."

"I feel peculiar," the general confessed. "It's like something's hollowing me out from within. I feel hot and cold and … a ghost of myself. And it's not just me. The rest of staff is affected, too. And reports show the same is happening on Earth, although our telecom is off because a signal keeps intruding. Isn't that so, Doctor?"

"I've taken measurements," Dr. Lee observed, in the same, heavy voice as the general's. "The forces holding our atoms in place are starting to weaken. If this continues, we'll literally fade to nothing."

Felix gulped. Everyone alive was a walking paradox. Because Aceticus was dying, he might not finish his book. If his book weren't finished, Felix hadn't stopped the plague. That meant every soul around him had turned to dust the year before. They were living contradictions, no more, no less. Their atoms were coming loose because, if Aceticus died, they couldn't exist.

As if to prove this point, a screen was crackling. That signal that the general had mentioned was breaking in. It was 90 percent static, but an image lurked beneath.

"It's that damn signal," the general cursed. "It's been messing with our instruments these last few minutes. And it's only getting stronger. Have you any idea where it's coming from?"

"None," the doctor mused. He might have been speaking from inside a box. A thin line of blood was stealing from his ear.

Felix took a good look at the screen. He could just make out a ghostly figure. Beneath the static he could hear the occasional phrase. He closed his eyes and focused …

"… created terrible havoc, delighting in war, savagery, and ignorance. But as often …"

He frowned. These words sounded familiar. Where had he heard them? He leaned back in and listened closely.

"… something rare and precious disappears — as light inevitably must dissolve into shadow. God bless us all …"

He narrowed his eyes and considered the screen. A silhouette was visible, shaky and dim. Then he sucked his breath in as the words gelled together. He was listening to President Gupta speak! In the world where he hadn't found the *lupus ridens*, Gupta had spoken before the plague had killed him. His speech had been broadcast all over the world. The signal was coming from this alternate future. The closer Aceticus got to death, the more this future was dislodging their present; very soon it might take over their time frame completely.

"Where are you going?" the general asked, as Felix ran to an exit.

"I'm checking on Aceticus. If he's conscious, he'll need reassurance. After all, those Health Drones can't speak Latin."

"Go ahead." The general sighed. He raised a shaking hand to the light. By now his skin was partially transparent.

Felix walked to a door at the far end of the room. On its surface was written OR 3. The door slid open and ... there he was. The old man was lying on a peculiar bed. Its surface could be lowered and raised, but its base was box-like and resembled a coffin. Its hollows were probably a storage space. Above it was a shelf with small blue orbs — these were portable memory disks. A line of them was labelled CM I-VI.

But the old man was his first concern. Much to his amazement, Aceticus looked stronger. A surgery team had "sealed" his artery, repaired the cuts his organs had sustained, and fused his wounds without leaving a scar. It had replenished his fluids and injected him with meds. His pulse was strong and his colour was normal.

"How's the patient?" he asked the closest surgical drone.

"He will recover. But he could use further repairs. His blood sugar and cholesterol are high, his bone density low, and his liver contains toxins. His teeth, too, are worn ..."

"Never mind," Felix said, unwilling to extend the old man's natural lifespan. "No maintenance is required. When will he be ready for TPM transport?"

"Based on his hemoglobin," the drone replied, "one hour and sixteen minutes."

Felix looked at a Teledata screen. It was full of static still, but the signal was weaker. Because Aceticus had been saved, they'd gained themselves time, but they weren't clear of the danger yet, not by a long shot. They had to send the old man back, fully committed to writing his book. The question was how.

Aceticus was conscious and agog at his surroundings. His eyes were wide and he was full of questions. "Am I dead?" he asked. "What are these devices? And what is the meaning of this gadget on my skull?" He was speaking Latin and the drones couldn't answer.

"*Salve, magister*," Felix greeted him. "You're looking better."

"Where am I?" Aceticus groaned. "And why did you keep me from dying?"

"We're in the future," Felix said, without beating round the bush. "The Rome you know has long since vanished."

"What are you saying?" Aceticus wailed. "That it isn't **683** *ab urbe condita*? And Lentulus and Orestes are no longer consuls?"

"It has been **2,967** years since the city's founding. There is no such thing as consuls now. And to answer your question why I saved your life, billions of people depend on you. If you die, they'll die, too."

"Do you think me a fool?" the old man exploded. "Do you think I don't know a lie when I hear one?"

"*Domine*, please. You'll open your wounds!"

"Stop pretending that you care for me! You took away my will to live when you proved how paltry my efforts are! Leave me be and let me sink into the shadows!"

When the old man paused to catch his breath, Felix tried explaining again. He repeated that Rome had turned to dust and that the world had made much progress since, to the point that people could visit the past. He added that these achievements would die and humankind languish if Aceticus didn't finish his book.

"It's hardly a book," he said. "It's the scribblings of a wretch."

"It isn't. I've read it. It's something to be proud of."

"If you've read it, then I don't have to finish it."

"You're mistaken, *domine*. If you don't write it, I can't possibly read it."

Felix and Aceticus stared at each other. To convince him of the truth of his words, Felix held his hand and was squeezing hard. It was cold to the touch, as if belonging to a corpse.

"Enough!" the old man shouted, yanking his hand free. "I don't know what your plan is, but you won't sway me with your lies! Send me back this instant! I find this place frightening. I'm not dead here, nor am I truly alive. As for that book, I won't write it! Do you hear? I'll die before I pick up a stylus! Why are you just standing there? Send me home!"

Felix had one last play to make. That's why he addressed Bernard, the Station's operating system. When a soft voice answered, he requested to be linked to the World Satellite Reconnaissance System. He asked to be joined to it by cognitive implants so that the images it relayed would seem all the more real. "We'll start in Toronto," he stated, "on the roof of my father's Book Repository."

These directives were barely out of his mouth when a chair appeared from out of the floor. When he was seated, a probe brushed against his skull and he felt mild pinpricks as the implants were installed. Through his Mem-gauge, Aceticus was linked already.

"WSRS hook-up in five, four, three, two, one ..." Bernard spoke, only to conclude with, "Online."

Felix was whisked at the speed of light from his place in the Station to a busy urban scene. He was on the roof of the Book Repository in downtown Toronto. Below him was a four-tier thoroughfare (once known as Yonge Sreet) and, off to his right, the new Nano-Center, the city's tallest super-structure, with its three hundred stories and iconic dome. Surrounding them were other towers, and the air was thick with shuttles and drones.

In actual fact they weren't on the roof, or anywhere else in the downtown region; their bodies were on the Station still. They were hooked directly into the system and this neurological link-up made them feel they were there.

"What is this?" the old man gasped. He was still just as angry, but sounded deeply impressed.

"It's a city called Toronto," Felix said. "It's home to over ten million people. Do you see those flying objects?"

"They are like enormous birds, only much more beautiful."

"Those are transport devices, winged chariots, if you will. Each can circumnavigate the globe in fifty minutes, with a thousand passengers inside its belly."

"These towers," Aceticus asked, "they are higher than Olympus. How do they stand?"

"They are made from a metal much stronger than iron."

They kept watching the scene. In the distance, a communications tower was under construction: service drones were zipping all over, transporting materials, welding these in place, installing circuits, and performing a thousand other functions, dozens of them, hundreds, all working together. In the streets, other drones were inspecting the roads, repairing cracks or zapping debris. Every window, every surface was clean enough to eat on, and the city, seen from a bird's-eye perspective, was like one gigantic animal, so synchronized and finely tuned were all its actions.

"It's beautiful," Aceticus said with a sigh. "Do machines perform all the work?"

"The physical work, yes," Felix replied. "Humans do other things." He didn't bother adding that these humans were machine-like, too.

"Where are these humans?" the old man asked. "The streets are almost empty."

It was true. Given the time of day, the downtown should have been packed. Instead there were few pedestrians about and those that appeared were clearly in trouble: they were walking unsteadily, if they were walking at all. Some had collapsed and were being assisted by Health Drones; others were barely able to manage. Felix assumed the people indoors were no less affected.

"It's as I said," he replied. "The population is sick. Those people you see are typical. They are dying, all of them, because you didn't write your book."

"That's nonsense. You can't blame me for this. You may as well blame Romulus for Spartacus's mutiny."

Felix didn't answer. There was no sense arguing, not when he could take a different tack.

"Let's visit Rome," he said. "But you're in for a shock. Rome, the ancient forum," he ordered Bernard in Common Speak.

The scene changed drastically. One moment the Toronto skyline was before them; the next they faced a stretch of ancient ruins. The contrast·was so sharp that even Felix was impressed.

"What is this?" Aceticus asked. His voice was suddenly dry with emotion.

"I think you know," Felix said. "Those columns joined by an architrave? They're all that's left of the Basilica Aemilia."

"On the right, is that the temple of Vesta?"

"Yes. It's recognizable still. And you see those other ruins? That arch, the *curia* house, and that pitted structure belonging to some *thermae*? They were built long after you were alive. Not that it matters. Rome collapsed eighteen hundred years ago. Only a tiny part has trickled down, the very best the city produced. I'll show you an example of what I mean."

As Aceticus looked at the ruins in shock, Felix told Bernard, "Toronto, Area 2, Sector 4, Building 9. Place us in unit 2103, please."

A moment later they were gazing at the Taylor home. Instead of the usual tidiness, the place was a mess. The windows contained two gaping

holes, shards of metal littered the floor (from the
Enforcement Drones Felix had crushed), a shelf was
overturned, and books lay everywhere. The stone
from Ganymede was lying on the couch. While this
disorder was shocking, he couldn't dwell on it then;
instead he called to Bernard.

"Can you restore the Domestic System? Its
power source was neutralized."

"Repair protocols established," Bernard replied,
a split second later. "Power is restored. 3L Domestic
Service, nicknamed Mentor, is back online."

"Thank you," Felix called. "Mentor? Can you
hear me?"

"I can," a familiar voice spoke up. "Welcome
home, Felix. You are cognitively linked to the WSRS,
I believe?"

"That's right. Listen. Can you find Aceticus'
Historiae? It was in my dad's study when I saw it last."
Even as Felix posed this question, he could see that
Mentor was tidying the unit. The holes in the window
were being sealed, retractable arms lifted the shelf off
the floor, and the metal shards were being swept away.

"I have found the book, Felix. I have returned it
to your father's desk."

"Thanks. Can you open it to the first page and
direct our gaze above it?"

No sooner had he spoken than they were eyeing
the book. Its pages were brittle and yellow with
age, the signatures were coming loose, but overall
the book was in fair condition. And as Felix had
anticipated, Aceticus was reading the opening page.

"These words are mine?" Aceticus said, after a minute.

"When Rome collapsed, a small fraction of its texts survived. Yours was among them."

"Incredible," the old man marvelled. "This print is so beautiful, so sharp and crisp. And my Latin isn't so terrible, is it?"

"It's not just the style, *magister*, but the contents, too. Of all the books that have survived the ages, yours is easily the most important. This new Rome won't survive without it. There are twelve billion new Romans at large; all will turn to dust this very day, if you don't write your *Historiae*. Our future rests in the tip of your stylus. Bring us back," he told Bernard, "and log us off the system."

"Logging off," Bernard replied.

Before they could draw a single breath, they were back in OR 3. After blinking several times to adjust to the change, the old man gazed at Felix. His anger was gone and he was smiling shyly.

"I know what must be done," he said. "I will finish my *Historiae*. I swear this by Clio, the muse of history."

Felix nodded and thanked the old man. He then addressed the surgical drone.

"Is he ready for the TPM?"

"Yes."

"And have you tracked his memories since his arrival here?"

"Yes. All recent memories have been registered."

"Including his promise to complete his book?"

"That is correct."

"Then implant this last memory and delete the rest. And administer a sedative. He must not remember his journey back."

Felix just had time to squeeze the old man's arm before a sedative invaded his veins and he dropped off like a baby. With no time to waste, Felix told the Health Drones to return the historian to the TPM.

Aceticus was soon lying in the see-through sphere. Its gases were swirling into a black discontinuity — the start of the wormhole that Felix had created. Stroking the old man's cheek one final time, Felix said, "*Pax tibi*." He then retrieved his figurine and, exiting the sphere, pressed its base and sealed the wormhole closed. Aceticus vanished in a puff of smoke.

Again Felix gasped. Alive and breathing a minute before, the historian had now been dust for over two thousand years.

Chapter Eleven

Ten minutes had passed since the Roman's jump to the past. To his surprise, Felix discovered that, in all that time, he hadn't moved a muscle. His eyes were half-closed and his breathing was uneven. The general and doctor were poised by the console and just as reluctant to stir as Felix, as if the slightest move might reduce them to dust. What if Aceticus hadn't written his book? Maybe its absence was taking shape in later eras, the Dark Ages, the Renaissance, the Enlightenment, the Belle Époque, the Great Depression, the TV Age, the Religious Wars, the Great Reforms. Maybe these were falling like dominoes and, any moment now, the last "brick" would totter and flood the present with the plague's effects. In ten seconds, five, people's atoms would melt and Felix would be the last man standing....

Another minute passed. The silence was deafening.

But the general and doctor existed still. Their eyes were glued to a Teledata screen, and, while neither showed the slightest emotion, they weren't shaking as much and their bodies seemed stable. Their hair, too, was back to normal. So maybe they were there to stay.

Felix took a step. When the world didn't end, he took another, then another. Emboldened, he moved away from the sphere, climbed some stairs, and joined the pair.

"Are you okay?" he asked.

"I'm fine," the general answered, daubing at some blood that had escaped his nostril. "I might look terrible, but at least that weird inner quirkiness has passed."

"Readings show our atomic 'glue' is stable," Dr. Lee pointed out. "I guess that means the Roman is back in his time frame."

"Of course he is," the general said. "And that rogue signal has vanished, as well."

"Pardon me general," Bernard broke in, "but all three of you could use caloric input. And Felix should be hydrated."

"Thank you, Bernard," the general said. "This way, gentlemen."

On legs that were still wobbly, the general led them across a catwalk to his office. The only piece of furniture was a Lignica desk whose surface was empty but for a hologram of Carolyn. It showed her as a girl, without ERR: her features were relaxed and her smile was full.

Felix gulped. She was all alone.

"Sit," the general said, pointing to a pair of seats that had risen from the floor. "Nutrition," he barked. Felix was used to Mentor, whose circuitry was old. It surprised him, then, when a port swiftly opened and three glasses with a pink, viscous liquid appeared.

The general nodded, encouraging them to drink. Lifting his glass, Felix took a sip. While it wasn't as tasty as the meat from last night, it did provide him with a feeling of well-being. Not only did his energy increase, but his mind was suddenly sharp and focused.

"All right," the general sighed, regaining his strength as well. "The first threat's over. What's next on our plate?"

"I've got to get to 2111," Felix said. He briefly described the assassin's attack and how, despite their efforts, he'd made good his escape. On the off chance the "child" was heading for Stockholm, Carolyn was pursuing him there. Felix planned to join her, the sooner the better.

The general nodded. While he wasn't happy that his daughter was alone, he appreciated the need to follow the killer. He asked the doctor if the date and place meant something special.

"Indeed they do," the doctor spoke. His body was normal, but his face was still pinched, as if he were fighting an affliction that would never let him be. Even a year after the fact, with ERR to smooth things over, his son's abrupt death still tormented him. "The 'child' is headed for 8 Haymarket Street, in Stockholm. This address is where its famous Concert Hall stood."

"A concert hall?" the general asked. "I don't know what that is."

"It's a building where people called 'musicians' would gather. They would play various instruments: violins and objects you sometimes see in museums, as an audience listened in."

"You must be joking," the general said, then snorted. "That sounds insane."

"I've seen films of this. It's very odd," the doctor replied. "But never mind that. In addition to its orchestra, this hall hosted the Nobel Prize festivities."

"I've heard of those," Felix broke in, glad to escape the subject of music. If these men found out that he listened to recordings, for sure they'd think that he was touched in the head. "They were awarded to great scientists and other thinkers. They were prestigious in their day."

"I see," the general said. "Why is that 'child' travelling here?"

"On December 10, 2111," the doctor explained, "a Nobel ceremony is scheduled to take place. Among the winners is a familiar name: Johann Clavius."

"The same Clavius behind the TPM?" Felix asked.

"Through his unified field equation, yes. But that was published later, in 2165. He's also the 'father' of accelerated cloning, chaos theory, and neuro-mapping. This last field led to memory deletion and ERR. In fact, it was for his work in neuro-mapping that he won a prize in 2111."

The doctor paused to let his words to sink in. The three sipped their drinks in silence. Whereas the general was nodding his head in approval, as if to say he admired Clavius greatly, Felix wasn't sure what to make of the giant. Sure, the guy was brilliant, but had he really made the world a better place? Had ERR created as many problems as it had solved? Not that it mattered. "Why would Clavius interest the killer?" he asked, voicing the more crucial question.

"That's what I was wondering," the general agreed.

"Bernard, bring up photos of Johann Clavius, please," the doctor replied. Moments later, several holograms appeared alongside Carolyn's. One showed Clavius as a ten-year-old boy, blue-eyed, blond-haired, and chubby-cheeked. He was posing with five trophies he'd won, in all the major sciences. Later shots showed a man in his twenties, with a distracted, haunted look. In one he was dressed in a Zacron tuxedo and wearing a medal about his neck — the Nobel Prize. The only other image was of a filthy hobo with a beard and wasted cheeks. The man in this photo was clearly dead when it was taken.

"You can see from these pictures," the doctor went on, "that there was a puzzling gap in Clavius's life, one in which he vanished from the public scene. In fact, it was just after this event in 2111 that he pulled up stakes and disappeared. For the next sixty years he lived alone in a hut. This picture shows his corpse when it was found, in 2173."

"He became a hermit?" Felix asked.

"Yes. He cut himself off from the rest of the world, without a word of explanation. Strange to say, this period was his most productive. It was when he was living in the middle of nowhere that he devised his theory of accelerated cloning, chaos computation, and unified theory. And there you have it. The life of a genius."

Again the doctor paused, and again the group drank. After a minute of silence, the general spoke.

"I'm sorry, Chen. I'm not following. What are you saying?"

"I'm saying the killer knows Clavius will be on hand to accept his Nobel Prize. After that, the genius will be impossible to find. If he's going to kill him, this date marks the perfect occasion; the only occasion, I might add."

"But why kill him?" the general demanded. A spot of the pink fluid was on his lip and, despite the serious tone at large, Felix almost smiled.

"Surely that's self-evident," the doctor replied. He pointed to the general's lip, to advise him of the spot. "If he kills Clavius, there'll be no unified field theory. No theory, no TPM. No TPM …"

"No time travel," Felix groaned.

"And again the plague rages. In other words, I'm afraid we're back to zero."

The general's face was like a totalium block as the doctor's reasoning hit squarely home. The single word "delete" was uttered and Bernard cleared away the scientist's photos. Only Carolyn's shot remained: was it Felix's imagination or was she giving him a wink?

"All right," the general said, "our mission is clear. We stop that killer by any means necessary. Do you hear me, son?" He was staring straight at Felix.

What choice did Felix have? "By any means necessary," he agreed.

"Remember. Three minutes. And every word will be recorded."

"Yes sir."

"I know he's your father, but he deserves no pity."

"I understand, really."

"And we have plans for him, just so you know."

"I'm just grateful for the opportunity, sir."

With a feeling of dread, Felix watched the general approach a retinal scan. Its beam verified that he was General Manes and there was a hum as the magnets on a door disengaged. The totalium slab opened and Felix stepped into the space beyond.

It was large and dimly lit with ceiling pods. Three of its sides were nothing but metal; the fourth consisted of metal, too, only it was broken up into a series of windows. Beyond each Durex square was a prison cell. Of the five cells present, only one was filled. Felix stood before it and looked inside. As expected, he spied his father. Bernard had warned him that his son was coming, but his dad was lying like a lump on his cot, too dispirited to move or blink.

Unless guilt had him paralyzed.

"Vale pater," Felix spoke. Just as quickly he switched into Common Speak, so the general wouldn't think that he was plotting with his father. "It's good to see you although I wish these were happier times."

His father showed no sign that he was listening. Felix almost groaned. This was going to be even harder than he'd thought. "We have three minutes," he went on. "I was hoping you could supply me with your version of the facts...."

Felix placed his hand on the window. When his dad didn't follow suit, he lumbered on.

"Let me ask you this. Are you plotting to bring the plague back? A simple no or yes will do."

Nothing.

"We're high up on a space station. It contains the TPM — a top-secret time machine. Someone flew here in a CosmoComm shuttle, the one we took to get to the Space Hub. This person forced a scientist here to send a killer to the past — we can do this now. He happened to leave a pencil behind and some fibres from a Zacron suit. These details suggest you were that guy. In fact, that scientist fingered you when he saw your picture. It looks like your guilt is written in bold letters, but maybe you can explain this stuff."

There was still no response. If anything, his dad seemed more removed than before. His silence angered Felix. He spoke again, almost shouting this time.

"I've seen the full effects of the plague. If it runs unchecked, it will kill everyone! Not a single soul on the planet will survive."

He stared long and hard at his dad. It was unbelievable. He was being told his guilt was obvious yet he didn't seem to care. This was absurd; no, it was ... monstrous. To hear this news without batting an eye meant he was more cold-blooded than Felix had dreamed. He yanked his hand away from the window.

"I've always admired you," he said. "It's why I took the classics to heart. But if I stop the killer and keep the plague from recurring, I swear I'll never touch a book again. If your learning can push you to act like a brute, then there isn't any value to such ancient wisdom."

A light signalled his visit was over. He wanted to tell his father that he'd always loved him, and that his very best moments had been spent by his side, but he couldn't get a word out. Instead he turned and retraced his steps to the entrance. Crossing the room's threshold, he heard the totalium slab close behind him.

It was as if a lid were slamming shut on his father's coffin.

"Are you all right?" the professor asked with an anxious look.

"Yes," Felix said mechanically. "Actually no. I saw my father."

"I'm very sorry," the professor said. "That can't have been easy."

They were sitting in his office and preparing for his jump to Stockholm. The next best time for TPM engagement was an hour from then, and they were hurrying to get certain details arranged. Once again the professor's cabinet door kept swinging open. As they spoke, it kept banging MacPherson on the skull and he kept closing it with a look of impatience.

"I can't believe he's plotted something so destructive."

"I hate to say this, *fili mi,* but the evidence is damning...."

"I know. I'm not saying he's innocent, only that he's not the man who taught me Latin."

"Maybe you never saw this side," the professor ventured. "Our obsessions can sometimes colour our judgment. If you engage with the past the way your father has, constantly spurning the ways of the present, I imagine the effects can be unhealthy at times."

"I suppose," Felix said listlessly. He didn't smile as the door swung open yet again.

"Yes, well, let's get on with our planning." The professor sighed, aware that he couldn't comfort Felix. "You have your Kevlar outfits, correct? One for each of you when you track down Carolyn?"

"Yes," Felix said, pointing to two bundles of clothes. "Was this really the style back then? To wear bulletproof fabrics?"

"I'm afraid so," the professor said. "The period was difficult and violence was common. And I hate to repeat myself, but I'm very impressed with your English and German. Your father certainly taught you well."

They were conversing in early languages called English and German, which had been common back in 2111. Felix didn't speak Swedish, the language of Sweden, but these other languages would serve him well.

"Thank you. You mentioned a means of exchange. I assume you don't mean cinnamon?"

"No. It had no value in 2111. But I've provided you with something that does." He motioned to a leather pouch.

"What is it?" Felix asked, wrinkling his nose. The package gave off an acrid smell.

"It contains tobacco. I could provide you with some paper money, but no one would accept it. Instead the population trades in gold or silver — a sign of the wars at large. The TPM can't handle metal, so I've given you tobacco instead. By 2111 tobacco was outlawed and hard to obtain. That means it's worth a fortune now, although by trading it you'll be breaking the law. I'd much prefer this wasn't the case, but we're in a jam and can't afford to be fussy."

"By any means necessary," Felix murmured aloud.

"Quite. Remember, too, your belts are now your ticket home. The buckle is charged and will return you here. Personally I liked those statues, but they'd draw too much attention in 2111."

"The doctor explained everything," Felix said.

"There's one last item," the professor mused, flinching as the cabinet door struck him again. "What was it…?"

As he tried to recall the final point of business, Felix's eyes strayed to the cabinet. He idly observed its contents: books, two suits, a spare pair of glasses, decorative items …

"Oh, yes," the professor said, remembering suddenly. "The scan vans. You must be sure to avoid these contraptions." With a frown, he closed the cabinet door and leaned his chair against it.

"Scan vans? What are those?" Felix asked.

"In 2111, ERR was catching on, courtesy of Clavius' neuro-mapping. At the same time the religious wars were at their height. Some people put two and two together. They believed ERR could change religious folk into *rats* like themselves."

"By *rats* you mean rational types, correct?"

"That's right. The *theos* — that was what they called the religious people — believed ERR was a terrible idea. Both sides roamed about in 'scan vans.' These were vehicles equipped with neuro-implants that could either remove ERR or install it at will. Depending on whom you run into, you'll be their friend or their worst enemy. These are very dangerous times and you must exercise caution."

"I see. I'll do my best to be careful."

"I'm afraid that's all I can do for you, *puer*. Good luck and remember …"

"Yes?"

"Forsan et haec olim meminisse juvabit."

While Felix detested all this talk of *theos*, *rats*, and "scan vans," he couldn't help but smile at this Latin reference. Shaking hands with MacPherson, he left his office, comforted by the line from Virgil. He repeated it aloud and savoured its meaning.

"One day it may be pleasant to remember even calamities like these."

Chapter Twelve

"*Se upp grabben!*" a deep voice growled.

Felix opened his eyes. A moment before he'd been orbiting Earth on a Class 9 station; now he was standing in the *tunnelbana*, the subway system in old Stockholm, and a man was bearing down on him with a giant dog. Flanking him were magnorails, which were an improvement on the diesel engine, but way less effective than Dispersion Portals. The station's tiles and ceiling lights were also signs of an earlier era.

"*Se upp grabben!*" the man repeated. His dog was growling and baring its teeth. Felix didn't know dogs well, but his instincts told him that this beast meant trouble. Nodding tersely, he stepped aside. As the older man passed, he glared at Felix, as if he were tempted to bite him, too.

His hostility suited the atmosphere. The floor's tiles were cracked and covered with grime, half the ceiling lights had been badly damaged, and paint marks covered most of the walls. While he'd read about graffiti, he'd never seen it firsthand. It seemed to be the work of angry people.

People. They were loitering about and seemed far from friendly. Meanly dressed and sallow-faced, they looked badly fed and poorly cared for. Felix was used to a public show of coldness, but the citizens of his age lived in well-run cities and enjoyed maximum comfort, unlike this mob which looked severely deprived. They also looked cruel enough to do something about it.

He spied an exit to the main street. In a dim-lit stairwell that stank of misery and urine, he passed three men who were quietly chatting. They hailed him in Swedish. Felix shrugged and moved along. Without warning, one guy grabbed hold of his knapsack. At the same time his pals shone two blue lights into Felix's eyes. There was a glint of steel: they were carrying knives.

Felix broke free of the guy clutching his knapsack. He was going to lay him flat with his elbow when suddenly the trio started to laugh. One of them pulled his jacket open and disclosed a medallion on a fragile chain. Felix saw it was shaped like a cross, which he knew was a sign for people called Muslims; unless he was wrong and it signalled that other group, Christians. Religion meant nothing where he came from and he couldn't always keep the worshippers straight.

"Vänner," the knife guy said. *"Theos."* That said, the trio retreated from the stairwell.

Felix fled before they changed their minds. He realized that they'd let him go because their blue lights were scanners and had told them he was ERR-free. This meant they thought he was a worshipper like them, and not an enemy *rat*. Not that this was comforting. If these guys could attack the *rats* they met, then *rats* would be willing to assault them in turn.

Felix emerged from the subway. The outside scene was bleak. While it was minutes after 3:00 p.m., the dark was falling quickly. The sun was veiled in cloud and hovering near the horizon. He knew the days were short up north, during winter at least, but had never guessed they'd be as short as this.

The dark didn't bother him as much as the snow. He'd encountered snow on the rare occasion, but the Global Weather Template never let it stay for long; after a day it was always cleared from the system. Unlike here. The sidewalks were thickly coated with slush and the drifts by the curb were two feet high. Trees, signs, vehicles, and awnings, every flat surface held a layer of white, as if a shroud had been yanked over the city.

It might have been pretty if not for the blight. Felix was on a main street, with a square to his left. Around him was a line of buildings with elevated walkways visible in the distance, built from stone and nicely arched. Once elegant, these structures had been hammered badly. Massive chunks had been gouged from their sides, the doing of tank shells and other explosives. One walkway seemed on the brink of collapse. And on every building windows were gone, replaced by wooden boards. Most doors consisted of metal slabs with rolls of razor wire everywhere. The storefronts were empty, burned-out shells: fires had chased the merchants out. Every tree on the street was an ugly stump, and abandoned mini cars were scattered all over, their windshields smashed and interiors melted. There wasn't much light to dispel the darkness: of the light orbs hanging in the middle of the street, a mere third of them were functional.

Felix felt sick. He'd known this era had been difficult, what with the ruthless wars between the different religions, which had morphed into a war between the *theos* and *rats*, but he'd never guessed that it had gutted cities like Stockholm. The cold stole into him, despite the warmth of his clothes. Pulling the collar up on his jacket, he turned toward the concert hall.

Just as his spirits were entering a tailspin, Fate handed him a bone. While the cold scoured his face, and the snow teased his shoes, he heard a familiar voice cry out.

"F-F-Felix!"

He turned. Across the street was Carolyn. She was standing in a cone of light with darkness all around her, as if stuck on a raft which the sea was bent on sinking. She was breathing hard, her face was scratched, and her *palla* made her stick out in a crowd. Still, the sight of her was thrilling. Emotional displays weren't a good idea, but Felix couldn't help himself. Running into the street, he broke into a smile.

"I thought you wouldn't show," he said, as soon as he joined her.

"I g-g-got de-de-delayed," she replied. A wind was trying to steal her cloak and her legs were all exposed. Besides the cloak, she only had a tunic. She wore sandals instead of boots. Her toes were blue and she was shivering all over.

"You're freezing," Felix said. He slung the knapsack off his back and pulled out a jacket. "Slip this on. I have clothes you can change into when we find some shelter. And we'll get you something hot to drink."

"Gr-gr-great," she stuttered. Like her toes, her lips were partially blue. The scratch on her cheek was deep and the blood had frozen over.

Once she'd put the jacket on, Felix took her arm and scanned the street. There. Two blocks down was a "floating" sign. These were large block letters with tiny engines that allowed them to hover about in mid-air — it was a form of advertising in 2111. Taken together, the letters spelled "Nobelcafe." While cafés didn't exist in his own time frame, Felix thought this place would suit them nicely.

"There's a place down the road," he said.

"H-h-hurry," Carolyn chattered.

As they passed other pedestrians, they drew some stares. While most citizens were indifferent, the older ones were concerned. A wrinkled lady gestured that he should get her somewhere warm. He suspected that the difference between these nice types and the cold ones was ERR. He wanted to tell Carolyn this but, seeing her shivers, knew it wasn't the time.

There were also lots of policemen about. They were heavily armed and dressed in body armour. Their heads were helmeted and visors masked their faces. Each was brandishing a pulse gun and the sight of such weapons was hardly reassuring. The cops barely noticed the pair.

A short distance away, they came upon a square. Its cobblestones were badly cratered, from explosives, he assumed. At one end stood a blue, fortress-like building with a classical facade and Corinthian columns — the concert hall. Immediately in front of it was a group of sculptures; their heads were missing. An army of cops had gathered here: the Nobel awards were a really big deal and the city was making sure they wouldn't be disrupted.

A bee-like buzzing was suddenly audible. Pixellators filled the air. Massing together in different patterns, they formed 3-D portraits of the year's Nobel laureates. They were sculpting Johann Clavius just then.

"We're in the right place," Felix said, as he continued ushering Carolyn forward.

"All th-th-these m-m-men w-w-with g-g-guns. W-what's g-going on?" she stammered.

"I'll explain later." Felix was frowning. Given all the cops on duty, it wouldn't be easy to slip inside. "Let's focus on getting you warmed up first."

A minute later they entered the Nobelcafe. Unlike other stores, this place was normal, charming, even. It had lavish chandeliers, excellent heating, and was tastefully painted in blue and yellow, Sweden's national colours. The walls contained a series of screens that flashed the portraits of past Nobel winners. Delicious smells wafted about and the tables were filled with well-dressed people. The women were wearing elaborate gowns, while the men were sporting Zacron tuxedos. This show of formal dress implied these diners had tickets to the awards ceremony.

"Kan jag hjalpa er?" a heavy-set man in a tuxedo asked. The owner. While his suit was as fancy as everyone else's, he was toting a pistol beneath his jacket. The café might be charming, but was subject to attacks.

"Do you speak English?" Felix asked.

"Of course," the owner answered.

"Good. Could we have a table for two, please?"

"This is a select crowd. Admitting you is out of the question, I'm afraid."

"You must be kidding. My friend is frozen. You can't turn her away."

"That's where you are wrong," he said, with a shrug of indifference. Felix suspected he was equipped with ERR. "I can expel you if I choose."

Felix stared hard at the man. The man stared back utterly unfazed. He was about to call a waiter over but, before he could, Felix had an idea.

"Would it help," he asked, "if I had tobacco on hand?"

"Now *you* must be kidding," the owner sneered.

"You're right. I'm kidding," Felix said. He took out his pouch and showed him the contents. He poured a wad of it into his palm. "Can we have a table, along with food and drink?"

"I believe you're in luck," the owner replied, pocketing the tobacco swiftly. "But before we proceed, I must take a precaution." Here he took a wand from his jacket and swiftly waved it over their clothes. It was a metal detector that checked them for weapons. When its tip flashed green, the owner nodded. He also waved to a girl in a blue-and-yellow gown.

"This is my daughter, Aina. She will lead you to your table."

The girl curtsied and led them to a table in the corner. Carolyn asked Felix where the washroom was. He asked Aina who pointed to a nearby alcove. Handing Carolyn his bag, Felix took a seat.

He was feeling more relaxed. Carolyn was with him, they were safe and warm, and their objective was only five minutes away. The problem was the concert hall. How would they get inside with all those cops? They were dressed improperly and didn't have tickets. They could steal two tickets from the guests around them but first, this wouldn't be easy and second, they weren't properly attired. Even as he worked at this problem, his mind kept turning to Carolyn.

She was somehow different. Maybe it was her loneliness, her frozen state, or their adventures in Rome; whatever it was, she wasn't as cold. Her ERR was active still and she should have been distant. But there was no denying what his senses told him: she was friendlier and less inclined to snub him.

"This is a nice place," she observed, returning to the table. She was dressed in an outfit much like Felix's now. Her shivering had stopped and the dried-out blood was gone, though the scratches were still visible.

"What happened?" Felix asked, pointing to her cut.

"A Roman tried to grab me. It's weird how this cut is centuries old, huh? But I assume you were successful? Aceticus made it?"

Felix gave a rundown of the facts. He added that they knew why the "child" was in Stockholm. He'd travelled to 2111 because …

"Clavius will vanish after tonight," she said. "He's receiving a Nobel Prize for his work on ERR. But he hates the way his results are being used and will retire up north and live like a hermit. If someone's going to kill him, the time is now."

Felix gasped. "Wow, how did you know?"

"Because I read his biography and put two and two together," she said.

"It's interesting," Felix remarked, "that Clavius hates his invention. If he has doubts about ERR, maybe we should feel uncomfortable, too."

"You could be right," she said. "Maybe we've jumped to conclusions."

Felix almost grinned. He could have been talking to a different person. Two days ago she'd told him to accept the treatment and now she was willing to reconsider. He was amazed and was going to say as much, only a young man approached to take their order.

He was the same age as Felix, but looked older and more careworn. No wonder. Beneath his Zacron jacket, he too carried a pistol.

"I am Enar," he said, in halting English. "You have already bumped with my father and sister. What do you yearn to consume?"

"Choose something for us," Felix suggested.

"I will bring coffee and *fikabröd*. This is a sweet, most delicious snack."

"Fine," Felix said, smiling at Enar's stiff English. "That sounds great."

As he walked off, Felix glanced at Carolyn. She was eyeing him and her gaze was friendly. Her colour was normal and her spirits had returned.

"Your language skills are amazing," she said, "and that's not all. You're loyal and tenacious. I sold you short. When I arrived and was freezing cold, I didn't lose hope because I knew you'd find me."

"You're loyal, too. That's why you're here." He was blushing now. Her show of gratitude was shocking.

"I was following your example. I'm saying that I owe you an apology."

He couldn't believe it! She was holding his hand! Her mouth was open to say something further, but a commotion at the front door cut her short.

Some men had entered and were creating a ruckus. Their voices were loud and very angry and were followed by a high-pitched whine and a tinkling of glass. Struck by a pulse gun, a chandelier lay in pieces. The owner was trying to draw his gun, but before he could, a gun butt struck his jaw and he was writhing in pain on the floor. Some customers screamed and a tray toppled over. A voice called for quiet — or so Felix thought when the room fell silent.

"What's happening?" Carolyn whispered.

"I don't know," Felix whispered back. "It looks like people are robbing the place."

Six men dressed in police uniforms were standing at different points in the café. They were brandishing guns and pointing them all over. One of them, a giant moose of a man, was again yelling something at the room in Swedish. Four "cops" started scanning the crowd with blue lights in hand. When a woman closed her eyes, she was hit with a rifle and knocked to the floor.

"They're seeing if we're fitted for ERR," Felix said.

"How do you know?" Carolyn asked. She was clutching a fork. While she looked ridiculous, Felix knew she could use it. Her face was hard and her voice was drained of emotion.

"ERR is a big deal here," Felix murmured. "The *theos* hate it and worship God; the *rats* love it and believe in reason. When I was in the subway? Some guys scanned me with lights like these. Luckily they were *theos* and left me alone."

"What about these thugs? Are they *rats* or *theos*?"

Felix eyed them closely. By now they'd tested out half the crowd and found six victims who'd failed the test. These diners had been forced to their feet and escorted to the door. All looked frightened and three were crying.

"They're after people who are ERR-free." Felix gulped. "So they're *rats*, not *theos*."

"Will they nab you, too?" she asked.

There wasn't time to answer. Three men drew up

and aimed their rifles at them. Clutching Carolyn's chin, one thug scanned her eyes with practised ease. An instant later, he freed her with a grunt of approval. He then grabbed Felix who tried to drain himself of feelings. Hardening his features, he acted as if nothing fazed him, not the plague, not his mission, not his father's guilt …

He didn't fool anyone.

"We've got one," his "inspector" yelled — at least that's what Felix thought he said. Hearing this, the other two hauled him to his feet and marched him to the exit with the other victims. Carolyn made to intervene, but Felix signalled *no.*

As abruptly as they'd entered, the gangsters left, herding their victims out into the snow. Four ladies were wearing only their gowns and trembled in the cold. An older man skidded in a pile of slush, causing a guard to slap him roughly. The group was led a distance down the street until they reached an alley where a van lay waiting. A scan van, Felix guessed.

The leader halted and addressed his henchmen. They opened the double doors to the van, revealing two stools and two helmets dangling from the ceiling. These devices were more primitive than the ones back home, but their purpose was clear: they were neuro-implants. A woman wailed upon seeing them. Put off by her show of fear, the head guy searched for a calmer target. Spying Felix, he pointed him out. Two men pushed him to the start of the van. The leader spoke.

"I don't speak Swedish," Felix answered in English. "I'm from Toronto."

"You are Canadian," the leader spoke, in English, too. "Welcome to Sweden. When you leave our country, you'll be a different person."

"I'm not a *theo*," Felix said. "Where I come from, we don't worship any god."

"In that case, you won't notice if your feelings go missing. *Ta sig till arbetet!*" he called to his men. Felix assumed he was telling them to get to work.

"You have no right!" he yelled, as he was shoved into the van and slammed down on a stool. He tried to argue further, but a goon thrust one of the helmets down.

"We have every right," the leader said. "As men of honour, we must fix your wiring. If we don't turn you into a *rat* like us, you'll one day turn us into *theos* like you. And we're doing you a service. You'll see what the world is like when emotions aren't clouding your every impression." There was a metallic click as a switch was thrown.

The next few seconds were otherworldly. Felix's mind was suddenly clear and sharp as a computer. *Click click click*. These men would free him once the ERR kicked in. Otherwise why turn him into a *rat*? And Clavius? *Click click click*. He had to get into the concert hall. That meant … *click click click* … they needed tickets to get past the guards, but stealing them wasn't the best solution. So … *click click click* … they would have to disguise themselves as security men. This in turn would require them … *click click click* … to "borrow" uniforms from these *rats*. And once inside the hall…? *Click click click*. They would need nice clothes to blend in with the crowd. Where would they acquire these? *Click click click*. Enar and his sister were the perfect source. How would they procure them? *Click click click*. They could "buy" their outfits with the rest of the tobacco....

Even as his mind worked like a machine, he could feel something precious slipping away. Everything seemed sharper, yes, but far more removed. He didn't care that he was being handled roughly or that the tearful lady was set to go next. He didn't care about Clavius, or Carolyn and Stephen, or the troubling issue of his father's guilt. He felt no worry, no fear, no satisfaction. Wait. There was a glint of sadness, but suddenly ... it was gone. His emotions seemed like a sheet of light, which, with each passing instant, was receding further and further. There. It was a point in the distance. Any moment it would shatter and ...

It didn't shatter. Instead it hurtled back at him and trapped him in its folds. He felt all sort of stirrings, fear, concern, worry, jubilation. At the same time, hell was breaking loose outside. The ERR helmet was snatched away and tossed against the wall of the van. There were shouts and grunts and roars of pain.

He opened his eyes. He saw Carolyn punch the head *rat* in the jaw. Her leg knocked a second *rat* down, causing him to drop his gun, which she retrieved and pointed at the leader. His henchmen froze. They saw that she was fast and resistance was useless. When she motioned them to drop their guns, they did so quickly.

"Tell the captives they can leave," she yelled in Common Speak.

Felix shook his head. While he hated what these thugs were doing, he couldn't cause a butterfly effect. It was the "fate" of these *theos* to be turned into *rats*. At the same time …

"You said you're men of honour?" he asked the leader.

"We are," the man answered. "Not that you would understand…."

"I'll return your gun," Felix continued, realizing the weapon had a future of its own, "but you must give me two uniforms and swear you won't attack us."

"What about these *theos*?" The leader motioned to the captives.

"Treat them as you please." Felix said this coldly, but his guilt had him on the verge of puking. A lady overheard him. She wailed and her tears made him feel like a heel.

"Then I swear to abide by your conditions."

The exchange was concluded. A minute later, Felix and Carolyn were walking off, with two uniforms in hand. For their part, the *rats* were back at work on the *theos*. Two of them were being placed in the van, sobbing at the thought that they would lose their emotions.

Knowing he'd resigned them to their fate, Felix thought that he was guilty of murder.

Chapter Thirteen

The hall almost cracked apart as the Stockholm Philharmonic brought their performance to a climax. Horns, violins, trumpets, and drums blended together in one wall of sound, lifting the audience off their plush-lined seats. The roar was sonorous and brilliantly ordered, yet conveyed a wild range of emotion: rage and triumph and sadness and joy. While Felix had heard lots of music on disc, he'd never seen a live performance before and the effect was ... stupefying. He'd never felt so moved and had to wrestle back his tears.

His plan had worked out beautifully. After leaving the *rats*, they'd hurried back to the café where they'd swapped his tobacco for a tuxedo and an evening gown. They'd changed into the uniforms which they'd taken from the *rats* and hurried to the concert hall where they'd mixed in with the security staff. Getting inside had been a breeze. In a changing room, they'd slipped into their fancy dress: Carolyn had helped Felix with his tie, while he'd fiddled with the zipper on her gown. Finding two seats at the back of the hall, they'd watched the ceremonies slowly unfold. There'd been speeches, presentations, and lots of music. Felix felt paralyzed, he was so deeply stirred.

But he had a job to do. As the orchestra fell silent and the audience clapped, he scanned the hall for the hundredth time. Blue and yellow lights flooded the stage, which was crowded with dignitaries on throne-like chairs. Above them was a balcony with the Stockholm Philharmonic. Towering above the players was a massive organ whose array of pipes rose up to the ceiling, thick with spotlights, catwalks, and speakers.

The audience was standing. They numbered in the hundreds and looked … beautiful. The men were handsome in their black-and-white tuxedoes, while the women were stunning in their flowing gowns, the bright lights toying with their necklaces and bracelets. There were flowers everywhere, banners everywhere, and the hall was fragrant with soap, roses, eau de cologne, cognac, peppermint, chocolate, and perfume.

"What do you think?" he asked Carolyn. By now the audience had sat back down.

"It's very busy," she reflected. A moment later she added, "But it is spectacular."

"I'm glad we no longer go to war," he mused. "But why is there nothing like this where we come from? Why don't we have orchestras still?"

"They're impractical," she answered with a shrug. "Besides, the music is just a lot of stirred-up feeling. If they existed in our time, we would still be at war."

Felix was going to say what a pity this was, but a gentleman took centre stage and called for quiet. He was a tall, bearded man with a dignified bearing and had lines of medals pinned to his tuxedo. A near-transparent screen was lowered from the ceiling and floated just above his head.

"What's that screen for?" Carolyn whispered.

"I'm not sure. We'll soon find out."

"And why's he holding a stick?"

"It's a cane. He's old and uses it to help him stand. But shh, let's listen."

"Ladies and gentlemen," the old man spoke in Swedish. Instantly his words were translated on the screen, in English, Russian, Chinese, Arabic, Spanish, French, German, and Hindi. "That rendition of the New World Symphony was a fitting introduction to our next Nobel recipient, a young gentleman whose intellect is as rare as it is rarefied. Before receiving his award from our beloved king," here the gentleman bowed to a seated figure on his left, a clean-shaven thirty-year-old who smiled at the audience, "our young laureate would like to speak a few words. Without further ado, I give you Dr. Johann Clavius."

The crowd stood and applauded madly as a young man mounted the podium. Even from a distance, Felix recognized his features. Johann Clavius. His build was average and his face was plain, but the very air seemed to crackle around him, as if charged by the enormity of his scientific prowess. At the same time his posture was slightly bowed, as if he were shouldering a great disappointment.

Felix felt on edge, the way he would before a game of Halo Ball. Carolyn felt the same. She was sitting up straight and her muscles were strained.

"That's him," she said.

"Yes. Keep your eyes open. If the assassin's going to strike, it will happen any moment."

Carolyn nodded. Felix was surprised to see how focused she was. A moment before she'd seemed half asleep, whereas now her every sense was primed. He smiled at her. Again to his shock, she smiled back. She actually smiled.

"Your highnesses, ladies and gentlemen, fellow Nobel laureates," Clavius began, once the crowd had settled, "as you know I'm being honoured today for my work in ERR — a shorthand form for Emotional Range Reduction — which my research has made possible. While I can't express sufficient thanks to the Nobel Committee for awarding me this prize, I confess I suspect a mistake has been made and they have chosen someone who is most unworthy.

"In the past most discoveries have allowed humans to lead better lives. They have empowered us to produce goods cheaply, to travel places quickly, to communicate long distances, and to control our surroundings. My implants have had some benefit, too. The wars that began a century ago are showing signs of dying out, partially because ERR has tamed our passion and rendered combatants less likely to kill.

We are, generally speaking, a more rational lot, and as ERR spreads, peace will flourish. So far, so good."

He paused here and tugged at his collar, as if his tuxedo were like a noose about his neck. Felix felt sorry for the guy. He seemed hopelessly embarrassed and conscience-stricken.

"But over the last few months I've developed doubts," he continued, his milk-white hands rolled into fists. "While I've achieved my goals and curbed our worst habits, my fear is I have gone too far. I have cured the symptoms, but killed the patient. In many places, even here in Stockholm, ERR is being applied on an involuntary basis. The so-called *rats* are trying to 'convert' the *theos*, and the *theos* are out to 'liberate' the *rats*. And while the ERR protocols are narrow still, I fear there'll come a day when our emotions will be restricted further or, worse, they'll up and vanish altogether. Yes, violence will become a thing of the past, but so will joy, generosity, and exhilaration...."

As much as this speech dazzled him, something distracted Felix just then. It was a movement in a balcony just to one side. He studied the space. Yes! There was a flutter of a curtain and ... an arm emerged. And not just any arm. It was clothed in a rough, woollen cloak, exactly the garb you'd expect of a "guest" from Ancient Rome.

He poked Carolyn, who seemed equally dazzled by Clavius's speech.

"... efficiency counts for a very great deal," the scientist continued. "If we humans aren't efficient, the world can prove a very cruel place. But when efficiency becomes the sole measurement of progress, a different type of wealth gets lost. Art vanishes. Friendships lapse. Love, humility, and wonder disappear. Most frightening of all, to my way of thinking, our connection to our forebears gets lost in the shuffle and all their suffering and triumph are long forgotten, as though we owe these heroic souls not a whit, we owe nothing to the giants who made our existence possible ..."

"Carolyn," Felix hissed. "Over there." He motioned to the balcony. By now a good part of the figure could be seen — the head alone was steeped in shadow. Not only was he wearing Roman dress; in his right hand was a dagger, thin and vicious-looking.

The "child" assassin.

They stood simultaneously and hurried to an exit. In a whisper, Felix explained his plan. He would take the stairs to the second floor, hurry to the balcony, and catch the assassin unawares. He only had to activate his belt, grab his target, and the hunt would be over. Carolyn should keep watch here, in case the killer jumped and attacked Clavius on stage.

"Be careful," she warned him. "I saw a knife."

"I know. You be careful, too." Felix ran to a staircase. Peripherally, he saw Carolyn lean against a wall. A security man stood twenty feet away. Her intentions were clear. She wanted to watch Clavius, but to avoid the guard.

Moments later, Felix was on the second floor. A corridor faced him, lined with numerous doors. Behind each was a private box. The "child" was in the second one from the front and … there it was. Twisting his buckle to activate its charge, Felix grabbed the doorknob and took a deep breath. He opened the door slowly, just a crack. There. The killer was poised two metres away. Between him and Felix were two steel speakers. They explained why this box was off limits to the public. Clavius was still talking and coming in loud and clear. "… I'm proposing that we exercise caution. I'm proposing that we study the effects of ERR before we deploy it on a major scale. I also believe that we should restrict its use, to the workplace and our schools perhaps, and insist that citizens not lose sight of their emotions…."

Felix moved forward. The assassin had his back to him. At the same time all his sinews were tensed and his dagger was positioned between his teeth. He was just about to spring into action. If Felix was going to stop him …

"… do we wish to be machines? Is that our ideal? Do we crave the computer's purity of vision, unencumbered by what our emotions might say? I find this idea of humanity repellent and, to this extent, deplore my work on ERR…."

The assassin was on the ledge. He was inching forward. *It's now or never*, Felix thought, leaping at his target, one hand out and the other on his buckle. But a hidden bar on the speaker tripped him and at the very last instant the killer sensed his presence. On instinct, he turned and threw a punch, catching Felix on his shoulder. Felix's hand left the buckle, but he managed to grab the killer's cloak. Yanking hard he pulled the "child" down and used his weight to pin him to the floor. His left hand was on his buckle again, even as his right was trying to grip the killer's throat. The "child's" face was lost in the folds but, as he struggled and cursed, it jumped into focus.

Felix's mouth dropped open.

"What the...?" he gasped.

"Let me go!" a familiar voice yelled. "Quickly! She's about to strike!"

Felix was paralyzed. How was this possible? He was sprawled on top of … Carolyn! But he'd left her downstairs a moment before, so how had she managed to get there first?

"She's a clone!" Carolyn said. "The assassin is my clone! Get off me before —"

Two shots rang out. Screams immediately filled the hall, followed by the tumult of people scrambling. Carolyn — if it was Carolyn — lurched and threw Felix to one side. A second later she jumped from the box. As Felix stood he heard, above the crowd's wild screams, laboured rasps emerging from the metal speakers. Johann Clavius was struggling to breathe.

He scanned the space below. It was a mass of fleeing bodies. Hundreds of people were making for the exits and preventing the guards from entering the hall. As his gasps suggested, Clavius was lying on the stage, a pool of red expanding around him. The other dignitaries were running away and ushers were escorting the king to safety. The musicians were fleeing, except for a lone trumpeter who, in an effort to instil calm, was playing a fast-paced solo. The strangest sight by far, however, was directly below him.

Two Carolyns were locked in a life-and-death struggle. The one in the evening gown was swinging a rifle and trying to club her opponent. Her twin in Roman garb was brandishing a knife. The rifle butt caught her high on the side but she managed to roll and lash out with her blade. Blood appeared on her twin's left rib-cage.

"That's for shooting Clavius!" the Roman Carolyn cried.

"Killing me won't bring him back!" her twin retorted.

Felix was dying to help Carolyn — the real Carolyn — but Clavius was his priority. Being careful not to lose his footing, he climbed from his box to the one in front. He then leaped at a curtain, and, catching its folds, used it to descend to the stage. A second later he was kneeling by the genius.

His state was hopeless. The bullets had entered his chest and belly. His shirt was soaked a brilliant red, his body was shaking, and his guts were exposed. There was no way to convey him to 2214: to create a wormhole, he'd need a second portal and the real Carolyn wouldn't reach him in time. And even if he could jump forward, Clavius was beyond all hope of repair.

Within minutes he'd be dead. And once he expired, Felix's world would swiftly join him. He'd failed. Failed. Everyone would die. With a feeling of dread and bone-numbing sorrow, Felix took the scientist's hand.

"Who … are … you?" Clavius gasped. Remarkably, the physicist was conscious. Not only that. Despite his dying state, he was almost serene.

"My name is Felix Taylor. I'm afraid I've failed you."

"Failed … me? How?"

Felix hesitated. Should he reveal the truth — that he was from the future? Couldn't that trigger a butterfly effect? The sad truth hit him that it no longer mattered.

"I know this sounds crazy but I come from the future, the year 2214. A Temporal Projection Machine got me here, a device that was based on your unified theory. You haven't discovered this theory yet, but you will, or would have, if the assassin hadn't shot you."

"Why … kill … me?"

"Your theory will save the world a hundred years from now. The assassin wanted the future to fail and it looks like she's succeeded, I'm sorry to say." Here his disappointment proved too much. The world was over. Felix started to cry.

"You're … crying," Clavius said.

"It's over! I failed! A hundred years from now all of us will die!"

"No," Clavius said. With an immense effort, he raised his hand to Felix's cheek. Catching his tears, he held them to his eyes and studied them as if they were more precious than gold. He smiled widely, as if his wounds were nothing.

"Listen … Felix …" he gasped. "Unified theory … already … written. Papers … in … safety box. Lawyer … instructed … to open … sixty years. Your … world … safe."

"Are you sure?" Felix hesitated, worried he was being offered false hope.

"I … swear. Your … world … is … safe."

"I … I see." Felix gripped his hand harder. He could feel his pulse; it was getting weaker. The blood around him extended a metre. His trembling was violent and he was fading fast.

"Don't … leave. Company."

"I won't leave. I promise. And I'm sorry I failed you."

"No … matter. Lived … too long. And you … give … me … hope."

"Hope?" Felix asked. "What do you mean?"

"These," he gasped desperately. He was almost gone. "In … future … there will still … be … tears. Tears," he repeated. "Beautiful … like … rain."

His hand squeezed Felix's unbearably hard as his body struggled against death's embrace. And then it was over. A rattle sounded and the genius was dead.

Felix stood. If he could have, he wouldn't have moved for a year, but the police were coming and there was Carolyn to think of. With a frown of worry, he scanned the room. There. At the back. Both Carolyns were still fighting. They'd knocked each other's weapons down and were trading blows. The problem was they were evenly matched and neither could get the best of the other. They were gasping and on the verge of collapse.

"So it's over," the assassin crowed. Her gown was torn and flecked with blood. "I'm sorry I deceived you, but my mission came first."

"Murderer!" the real Carolyn rasped, with a bloody strip of the gown in hand. "I suppose we should congratulate you. You've just pulled the trigger on twelve billion people!"

"She did no such thing," Felix answered. "The unified theory is already written. Clavius's papers are locked away and will appear dead on schedule. Nothing has changed."

The assassin looked at Felix blankly. As the truth hit home, she rolled across an aisle, grabbed her rifle and rushed toward him. Before her "twin" could intervene, she held the gun to his skull. Their eyes met and he smiled slightly. He was too worn out to experience fear.

For several seconds she stood there, the gun at his head. Twice she made as if to pull the trigger. When a distant whistle sounded — a sign the police were near — she allowed the weapon to fall to her side. Much to his amazement (although nothing should have shocked him) she leaned in close and kissed his lips. An instant later, she was gone.

As the police came bursting in, their rifles at the ready, they were just in time to see two figures, a young man and woman, melt into thin air.

Chapter Fourteen

"**Y**ou should get that wardrobe fixed, Ewan. Or get rid of it altogether. It must go back three hundred years."

"More like four hundred, Isaiah. But it's no common wardrobe. According to the dealer I got it from — this is eighty years ago — this cabinet inspired a man to write a book for children. Like everything old, it's been long forgotten, but *The Lion, the Witch and the Wardrobe* was well-loved in its day."

"Loved or not, the wardrobe is broken."

They were seated with Professor MacPherson in his office, General Manes, Dr. Lee, Carolyn, and Felix. Two days had passed since their return from Sweden. As soon as they'd emerged from the TPM, Felix had described their "trip" then retreated to his quarters where he'd slept a whole day. Carolyn had followed suit after she'd been treated for some minor wounds. They'd eaten upon waking, received some shots, and were getting ready for the next confrontation.

"Let's get to it," the general announced. "You're telling me the assassin is Carolyn's clone?"

"That's right," Carolyn said. "It was the strangest thing, to fight myself. She predicted every one of my moves, as I did hers. The weird part is that she'd changed so much. When we met in Rome, she was ten years old, whereas this time around she was more my age."

"Accelerated cloning," Dr. Lee said.

"I beg your pardon?" the professor asked.

"Accelerated cloning," the doctor repeated. He was pale and his expression was more hangdog than ever. "If you choose the right medium, you can speed the cloning process. The years it takes to 'grow' an adult can be reduced to months or even weeks, except that there's a downside. The aging process can prove so rapid that the clone can't live for very long."

Felix frowned. Carolyn's clone was a menace, true, but like it or not, she was still Carolyn. It pained him to think that she would die so young.

"I'm just wondering," the general mused, "how my daughter was cloned. It's illegal, after all, and can't be easy ..."

"It's all too easy," the doctor replied, "once you have the right equipment. And even this isn't hard to acquire. The tricky part is getting cells from the victim. Once you have them, it's like baking a pie. I considered this idea, I must confess. If I'd had leftover traces of Charlie, I'd have cloned him without thinking, despite the law."

There was an awkward silence in the wake of his statement. The cabinet door opened and the professor slammed it closed. The noise returned everyone to the task in hand.

"How do you collect such cells?" the professor asked, rubbing his head where the door had banged it.

"It wouldn't take long. Did Mr. Taylor ever have close access to you, Carolyn?"

"I visited his house," Carolyn said. "Sometimes I fell asleep on the terrace. I guess I finally know where this mark comes from." She bared her shoulder and revealed the scar.

"That mark tells us everything," the doctor agreed. "And he would have recorded your memories using a Mem-gauge."

"Recorded her memories?" the general growled. Despite his ERR he was flushed and dangerous-looking, He clearly didn't like the idea that Mr. Taylor had probed Carolyn while she'd been sleeping.

"The clone's behaviour was like Carolyn's," the doctor said. "She must have her memories and these would come from a Mem-gauge."

"That's really creepy," Carolyn said.

"But where did the clone take shape?" the general asked. "I mean, even if Taylor had the right equipment, he couldn't grow a clone just anywhere."

"You wouldn't need much space," the doctor said with a shrug. "Just room for the cloning tank and the neural implants. Mr. Taylor runs the Repository, right? That must be where he created this clone."

The words stabbed Felix like a knife. He was thinking of that room in the Book Repository, the one his dad had made a point of locking. How had he explained this room? That it contained family skeletons he preferred to ignore? This had to be the place where the clone had been hatched. Felix felt his flesh crawl. His father was a monster.

The wardrobe wheeled open. The professor banged it closed.

"That makes sense," the general said. "Let's move on. The clone's next destination is Alexandria, 48 BCE. We need to determine why she's headed there. And there were four dates programmed into 'her.' The TPM allowed us to read the first three, but the code for the fourth is gobbledygook. We've got to discover what that fourth date is."

"We have a clue," Carolyn broke in with a leonine smile. "I tore her gown while the two of us were fighting and managed to bring a strip of it here. It's stained with her blood, which was programmed with a tracer. If we isolate the isotope …"

"We can calculate the target date!" the doctor cried. "That's very clever. Although the process can be complicated and I'm not terribly hopeful."

"Okay. Good." The general patted his daughter. "And Alexandria? Can you think of a reason why she'd travel there? Professor?"

"I'm not sure," MacPherson mused. "In the fall of 48, Julius Caesar's in the city. His army will meet the Egyptians in combat. But this doesn't tell us anything. How about you Felix? Any suggestions?"

"No," he replied. "I'm drawing a blank."

"Me, too," the doctor echoed him.

The group fell silent. As they looked vainly at each other, again the wardrobe door wheeled open. Felix again scanned the contents absentmindedly.... the suits, the books, the spare pair of glasses.... His blood suddenly froze. How odd. He had no idea the professor used ...

The general slammed his hand on the desk. The sound drew Felix's gaze from the wardrobe. The others were looking at the general, too.

"There's someone who does know," he declared. "After all, he's the one who created the problem. I'm talking about your father, Felix. It's time you paid him another visit."

"I did before I left. He had nothing to say. Another trip to his cell won't end any better."

"Except," the general said with a shark-like smile, "he's not in his cell. I'm proud to say I've delivered on my promise and found your father a different type of prison."

Felix was standing at the start of the Repository. He'd flicked on several lights and was gazing at an endless line of shelves. In front of him was his father's desk, with the speak-box, keys, and a pair of teacups. There were also six pencils, all lined up: the sight of them triggered a twinge of disgust.

It was a pity, really. Just days before, this place had been his deepest source of comfort. Because of his dad, it was now like a morgue. The books on its shelves seemed like rows of gravestones, marking ideas and stories that had longed turned to dust. If Angstrom wanted to close this space, Felix wouldn't stop him.

Someone coughed. It was a low, stifled rasp, but in that silence it sounded like a pistol shot. It reverberated up and down the shelves until, like everything in the Repository, it too turned to dust.

"Hello," Felix spoke. He was addressing a figure slumped over in an armchair.

"Hello, *fili mi*," his father answered. His tone was so hollow that his words seemed to die before they were formed.

"So you can speak again," Felix said. "I'm glad you're back to normal."

"I can speak," his dad replied. "But I'm not back to normal. They've seen to that."

Felix nodded. While he'd been off in Stockholm, General Manes had freed his dad, only to trap him in a worse situation. Mr. Taylor had been saddled with ERR, whose range was so impossibly narrow that his emotions were virtually non-existent. And with his emotions "zapped," Mr. Taylor posed no risk. This was why he was back in Toronto and "relaxing" with his books.

"Your position could be worse. You're in your favourite spot."

"Hah!" his father spoke. His tone wasn't bitter; it was merely hollow. "You don't get it, do you? By turning off my feelings, the general's robbed me of my interests. I'm surrounded by a million books, but the thought of reading them only turns my stomach. If his intention was to hurt me, he's achieved his goal."

He tried to smile. His muscles didn't fold the right way and the result was so hideous that Felix averted his eyes. He felt terrible for the man who used to be his father but …

"What did you expect? Of course he's out to hurt you, after what you've done."

"What have I done?"

"You need me to tell you? You don't remember hurting Dr. Lee? Or trying to awaken last year's plague? Or plotting to kill millions of people?"

"No."

"Really?"

"The doctor removed my latest memories so that he could scan them for clues. It's physically impossible for me to remember."

His father said this matter-of-factly. While Felix hated his neutral tone, and his dad's indifference to the disaster he'd caused, he realized at the same time he was telling the truth. His emotions were so whittled thin that he wasn't capable of lying.

"Well, how about this. Do you remember sending a killer to 48 BCE?"

"No. Can we do such a thing?"

"We can and you did. The question is why. What would your objective have been?"

"I don't understand."

"Let me phrase it differently. What happened in Alexandria on October 15, 48 BCE?"

"That's easy. Suetonius describes it. The library caught fire and burned to the ground. Hundreds of thousands of works were destroyed."

"That's right!" Felix gasped. "I should have known."

"But not everything perished. One part survived. It contained a mishmash of scrolls."

"A mishmash?" Felix asked. "Like Aceticus' work?"

"As a matter of fact, yes. All editions of his book can be traced to a scroll that somehow managed to survive this blaze. If it hadn't, we couldn't read him today."

"That's it!" Felix said. "That's why the clone's in Egypt. She wants to destroy the scroll so I can't read it down the road. That's your plan, isn't it?"

Felix tried to hide his fury as he asked this question. The more he thought of it, the angrier it made him. The entire world was poised on a cliff because his dad didn't like the way the world had evolved. Last year, when his father had died of the plague, Felix had thought the earth had stopped and wondered how he would ever continue. He'd even used the TPM to save his dad, not just because he loved the man, but because the world couldn't manage without his skills — or so he'd argued. The conscience of the modern age: that was how he'd viewed him. And now? He wasn't the world's conscience; he was public enemy number one.

The "public enemy" had his eyes on the ceiling. His expression was blank, but he was thinking hard. His knuckles were white, from gripping the armrests. Then suddenly he relaxed and glanced at Felix.

"I don't know if it's my plan," he mused, "because my memories are missing. But it's odd …"

"What's odd?"

"It's hard to describe. When I examine the memories in me still, I can't see any lingering trace of violence. You've said I'm planning something awful. It involves the plague and killing people. But there's nothing inside me that supports your suspicions. I see no evidence whatsoever."

Mr. Taylor said this calmly, but his words triggered an explosion.

"You want evidence?" Felix yelled, his voice full of rage. "I'll show you evidence! Come on! Let's take a walk!"

Approaching the desk, he grabbed a chain of keys. He turned to his father, seized his hand and yanked him to his feet. Ignoring the man's cry of pain, and the fact he was still weak from his confinement, Felix half dragged him down an aisle of shelves. When they reached its end, he veered to the left and hauled him down another murky aisle. At one point they passed several piles of books. His dad stumbled and fell against them. Felix didn't care. Still gripping his hand, he led him forward. By now his dad was breathing hard, but Felix didn't slow until they reached a door that was set into an alcove. Pointing to the lock, Felix turned to his father.

"In addition to your other crimes, you removed cells from Carolyn and created her clone. The doctor said it's easy. The equipment is basic and wouldn't require much space. You'd need a private room, that's all, like this one here. That's your secret, isn't it? That's why you've been careful to keep this room locked? While I was shelving books, you were cloning my friend."

His father was gasping too hard to answer. He was doubled over and coughing loudly. Snorting with impatience, Felix searched for the key that would open the lock. There were at least two dozen of them and they looked the same. One after the next they proved unsuccessful, and, as each one failed, his rage kept mounting. When the last one didn't work, he hurled himself forward, kicking the door and punching it until a hand restrained him. Fishing out another key, his dad placed it in the lock. The bolt turned instantly and the door wheeled open.

Panting still, he motioned Felix forward. With a bitter glare, Felix walked into the chamber. Groping for the light switch next to the door, he flicked it on and stared around him.

He was expecting to see a tell-tale tank, tubes, vessels, chemicals, and gadgets. In fact, the room was empty but for a shelf. This shelf contained one object alone: a dust-covered helmet. A tangle of wires dangled from its sides. These wires, and their contacts, could be plugged into a console. Felix inhaled sharply.

"That's an ERR unit," he observed. "Why's it here?"

His father was beside him now. He was gasping still and rubbing his leg. He looked old, frail, and beaten down. Even so, he took the helmet from its place on the shelf.

"Welcome to the museum of my youth," he joked.

"I don't understand," Felix said. His anger had left him and he was utterly spent. He'd been certain that he'd find a "smoking gun," to the point that he'd dared to treat his father roughly, and now ...

"I wasn't always a classicist," his dad explained. "As a matter of fact, I was extreme in my youth. I thought math and science were the only subjects worth knowing. I believed in logic and 'solid' thinking. I was a really big fan of ERR."

"No," Felix said disbelievingly.

"Oh yes," his dad insisted. "And I had it installed. It helped me focus when I was working. I was a structural engineer, you see. It was my job to demolish the old, worn-out buildings, which numbered in the hundreds decades ago, and make room for new totalium towers. When I toured these old structures I found furniture, appliances, art works, and ... books. Boxes of books, piles of books, shelves of books, rooms full of books. I destroyed dozens of libraries and millions of volumes. My method was simple. I'd pile all the tomes together, douse them with fuel and ... the flames were always thrilling."

While his father's gaze was locked on him, his pupils had a far-off look, as if they were reviewing these bonfires of old. It was funny. Felix and his father had spent years together and discussed every subject under the sun, yet he'd never once asked him how he'd come to love Latin or why he'd founded the Book Repository. Was this how it always was with people? You could know them well but only up to a point?

At the same time a thought was taking root.

"To make a long story short," his dad continued, "there was this one collection I'd just ignited. It was in a broken-down building and I figured what the hell. The flames were spreading when this woman comes running. Those books were hers, she yelled at me, and she couldn't let them burn. Before I could stop her, she dashed forward to save them, only she lost her footing and … to this day I can hear her scream. A book of Latin grammar was the sole survivor. That's when my outlook changed. I unplugged my ERR, mastered the classics, and atoned for my past by creating this Repository — the last of its kind."

"Why did you keep this ERR unit? And why didn't you tell me years ago?"

"The unit reminds me how lethal we are when we're drunk on logic. And I hid my story because I was deeply ashamed. These hands of mine? They've burned millions of books."

"They've saved millions of books, as well. You could have told me. I would've understood. As for logic …" He hesitated.

"Yes?"

Felix was looking hard at his dad. If he was sick at the thought of the books he'd burned, could he cause the deaths of millions of people? And

Fortuna   175

where was that supposed cloning equipment? His dad spent his days either here or at home. If the equipment wasn't here, or in their unit, maybe he wasn't linked to that clone. And if the clone wasn't his doing...?

"You mentioned logic," his father prompted him.

"Logic says you're guilty and behind these events. But maybe logic isn't the right tool to use."

"If logic isn't the right one, which one is?"

"I don't know. Fortuna maybe," Felix said, with a rueful grin.

"Welcome home, Felix. It's good to see you."

"I'm glad to see you too, Mentor."

"Can I get you something? You are short three hundred calories."

"Thanks, but no. I don't have time. I'm in a hurry and have a favour to ask."

"I will help in any way I can."

"I have a scrap of material here." Felix held out his hand. In it was a square of silk. It came from the clone's ripped evening gown. "It's stained, as you can see."

"My sensors indicate this stain is human blood."

"Yes. The blood contains a tracer that's been programmed with a date. Someone's already tracking it down, but a second pair of eyes can't hurt. Can you find out what this date might be?"

"Indeed I can. Estimated time for task: four hours, eighteen minutes, and nineteen seconds."

"That's great. In the meantime I've got to go."

"Will you be home for dinner?"

"I'm not sure."

He didn't add, as he left the apartment, that he might be delayed some two thousand years.

"Are you ready?" the doctor asked.

Felix merely nodded. He and Carolyn were on the threshold of the TPM and steeling themselves for yet another time jump. They were dressed in Roman tunics alone, as Alexandria was too hot for woollen cloaks and *togae*.

"Have you got your figurines?"

The pair checked their pockets and nodded. These figurines were crucial. If danger beckoned, they could return to the future and start their time-jump over.

"There's one slight change," the doctor said with some reluctance.

"What's that?"

"Your figurines have sufficient charge for just one person. There've been so many jumps in recent days that we can't provide you with a double charge, not without taking the Earth off-line."

"I see." Felix's mind was on his upcoming jump and he wasn't paying close enough attention.

"What I mean," the doctor said, in a gentle tone, "is that you can no longer capture the clone. There isn't sufficient charge to carry her back."

"You're saying we have to kill her," Carolyn spoke.

"Yes."

Despite his shock at this announcement, there wasn't time for debate. That's why Felix nodded and gave the doctor the thumbs-up. As he and Carolyn entered the sphere, and so the stream of time itself, he was thinking that they'd return as killers ... or they wouldn't return at all.

Chapter Fifteen

"**F**elix?"

"I'm here. Are you okay?"

"Yeah. Although I feel kind of woozy."

"So do I. Do you think you can take your leg off my chest?"

He and Carolyn stood. They were in a square chamber — the temple's *cella*. The room was spacious and two storeys high. It was built from marble with some gaps between its blocks, to allow the outside light to enter. Some of these blocks bore hieroglyphics — the Egyptians' sacred writing — but there was Greek writing, too. Before them was the statue of a man. He was thickly bearded, decked with a crown and carrying a staff with the horns of a bull.

Felix's head was clearing. They'd performed another time jump, he remembered. To judge by this statue, they'd arrived safe and sound.

"Where are we?" Carolyn asked. She was straightening her tunic. It left her shoulders bare and her scar was visible. Now that he knew it was from the cloning process, Felix felt embarrassed. Had his dad inflicted it, yes or no?

"We're in Alexandria, Egypt, in the temple of Serapis. That's his statue over there."

"Aren't lots of cities named Alexandria?"

"The name comes from Alexander the Great. When he founded a city, like this one here, he'd sometimes name it after himself."

"A modest guy, huh?" Carolyn sniffed. "So what's our plan?"

"We'll visit the library," Felix said, admiring the statue. He knew it wouldn't survive the past and wanted to remember it so he could draw it later. "It's about a mile from here. Once there, we'll lie in ambush for the clone and stop her in her tracks."

"That sounds easy."

"Yes and no. Alexandria is dangerous. A brother and sister are fighting over the throne. Caesar is here and supporting the sister — her name is Cleopatra. The locals don't like this. They feel he's interfering and the Romans should mind their own business. They're on the verge of war. In fact, the fighting will start later on tonight."

"Where does this leave us?"

"When the locals see our tunics they'll assume we're Romans. I can't imagine they'll welcome us with open arms."

"So we should stick to the Romans?"

"Not if we can help it. I'd rather not see Caesar. He might remember us from last time and that could lead to awkward questions. We should try to lie low if we can."

Felix moved away from the statue. Standing by a wooden door, he opened it a crack and glanced outdoors. The outside light was blinding and he blinked his eyes to get them to adjust. When he could absorb their surroundings he almost whistled.

Immediately before him was the rest of the temple, with its pillars and long stylobate. But the building was part of a larger complex. It was located in a spacious courtyard bounded on all sides by a roofed colonnade. The complex rested on a modest hill. At its foot lay Alexandria, the largest ancient city after Rome itself.

"Come on," he said, leaving the *cella*. "The coast is clear."

She followed and he closed the door behind them. Veering right, they proceeded to the compound's northern exit which would lead them to the Street of Columns, Alexandria's best-known thoroughfare. The sun flayed their skin and their sandals barely shielded them from the hot stone underfoot.

"It's boiling!" Carolyn said. "I've never felt such heat."

"It's noon. The heat is terrible, but it will keep the locals indoors."

As if to contradict him, they heard a burst of laughter. People were encamped in the colonnade's shadows to escape the fury of the noon-day sun.

They were there to make offerings to the god Serapis, but would do so when the heat relented. Some were napping, some were eating, while others were chatting affably together. Again a peal of laughter rang out.

"Why are they laughing?" Carolyn asked. They were halfway across the courtyard and her face and arms were dripping sweat. The heat didn't agree with her.

"I don't know," Felix answered, "but I think it's great. You don't hear laughter where we come from."

"You can't have laughter without misery," she said primly.

"I sometimes think it's a price worth paying."

"Did my clone like to laugh?" she asked.

"What?"

"My clone. Did she laugh when you were hanging together?"

"No. She was equipped with ERR. Her range was less constraining than yours, but not to the point that she would burst out laughing."

"You preferred her, didn't you?"

"What?"

"You heard me," she said, stopping abruptly. Grabbing his arm, she forced him to face her. "You liked her better than me. I saw you in the concert hall. You seemed cozy together."

"I don't know what you're talking about. And this is hardly the time …"

"She couldn't kill you," she said, in a disembodied tone. "She kissed you instead. She had no right. She should have asked my permission."

"Could we discuss this later?" Felix asked. At the same time he was wondering whether, beneath her ERR, Carolyn was … jealous? Was it possible she was jealous of … herself? If so, the irony was almost funny.

"I'm only saying this," she continued, defensively now, "because you can't let your feelings stand in the way."

"You mean, when the time comes to kill her."

"That's right. I have to know your nerve won't fail."

Felix was going to say that his nerves would be fine when they were suddenly interrupted. Carolyn had been shouting and her words had travelled across the courtyard. Perhaps it was the sound of Common Speak, unless it was their Roman dress; one way or another, they'd drawn people's notice and, from around the courtyard, a mob was forming.

"We have company," Felix said.

"So I see. Any suggestions?"

"Head to the exit, over by those columns. And try to blend in."

He said this as a joke. The pair was fair and garbed in Roman dress. The people around them had a different look: most were dark with short powerful builds. Some were wearing Egyptian dress, while others bore fashions with a Greek cut to them. Overall, they reflected the mixed population, Greek and Egyptian, with some Jews thrown in. There wasn't a single Roman about.

"Just keep moving. We're almost there."

He sallied forward, picking up his pace. Carolyn followed close behind. Their desire to leave only spurred the mob on. The ones behind them hurried forward, while others on the side converged on the exit, intent on cutting these foreigners off. A few succeeded. As Felix and Carolyn reached the edge of the compound, a dozen figures blocked their path.

"*Mi tatem!*" a burly guy yelled. "*Zi bousha litot kan!*"

"What's he saying?" Carolyn whispered.

"I have no idea," Felix said. "Let's see if this works. *Me sungchoirete*," he continued in Greek. "There seems to be some misunderstanding. My sister and I were admiring your temple and ..."

"You shouldn't be here!" the man thundered, speaking Greek as well. "This temple is reserved for Egyptians alone. There isn't any room for you overweening Romans ...!"

"We're not Romans," Felix explained. "We're dressed like them but —"

"— You Romans keep boasting how smart you are and how we Alexandrians are backward and stupid! Has it occurred to you that we're maybe happy with our culture and our views are as solid as your so-called reason?"

"That's very true," Felix said. He didn't dare turn round, but he sensed a crowd was closing in from behind. "Now if you'll excuse us, we're in a hurry ..."

"It's outrageous," the man continued, ignoring Felix. "You come here with your sense of order and think this entitles you to push us around. We don't want to be Roman. We don't want your laws and reason. We want you to leave us to our 'backward' ways!"

He shoved Felix. Realizing that the mob was about to explode, Felix gripped the man and flipped him over. At the same time, Carolyn cleared a path before them by knocking a knot of people down. Both shot forward before the crowd could nab them, and, darting past the colonnade, came upon a ramp. All of Alexandria lay before them and Felix yearned to study the view. But delay was out of the question. By now a hundred people were on the move.

"Run!" Felix said. "They'll kill us if they can!"

They stumbled down the ramp. Its angle wasn't steep, but its marble surface was smooth as glass. This meant they couldn't run all out. And their pursuers used their caution against them. Hurtling after them, some slipped and fell, while others came within an inch of their quarry. Felix threw a couple of punches. He hit one man and knocked him sideways and caused a boy to take a tumble.

They reached the ramp's end. Before them was an avenue, which was deserted on account of the heat. It was sixty metres wide, lined with soaring columns and displayed an endless length of buildings, some squat and modest, some impossibly grand. There were lots of shops with coloured awnings outside. Their owners were sprawled in front of laden stalls, with clothing, food, spices, and other wares on exhibit.

Shouts rang out. *"Romani, Romani!"* Instead of dropping back, as Felix had hoped, a dozen men pursued them still, in spite of the heat. Not only that. They were calling out to anyone who'd listen and urging them to join the chase as well. *"Romani, Romani!"* they screamed over and over.

Their shouts swiftly ignited the region. Spying the fugitives in Roman dress, people dropped everything and set off in pursuit. *"Romani, Romani!"* Faces appeared at doors and windows and, without pausing to ask what the chase was about, these strangers streamed outside, as well, until clusters of Egyptians filled the street. Some were armed. All meant trouble. *"Romani, Romani!"*

A stone went whizzing past Felix's ear. A pot fragmented a metre to his right: a shard grazed his leg and cut him slightly. A dozen oranges splattered around him: one landed squarely on the side of his head.

"Romani, Romani!"

He and Carolyn passed a troupe of soldiers — Egyptians, or so their uniforms suggested. At first these troops looked on in amusement. When they heard the crowd yelling, they decided to join in. One cast his spear, missing Carolyn by inches. A clatter reached Felix's ears. The soldiers' bronze was rattling as they followed behind.

"So ... much ... for ... lying ... low," Carolyn panted.

"Let's ... jump ... to ... Space Station," he gasped, pulling his charged figurine from a fold in his tunic. "Then ... start ... over ... again."

Carolyn nodded and drew her statue out, as well. But a stone struck her wrist and sent the figurine flying. It sailed through the air and landed behind some stalls. With a cry of frustration, Carolyn slowed.

"Keep ... going!" Felix yelled. "Too ... dangerous ... to search!"

As if to emphasize his point, two men drew near. Felix dispatched one with a roundhouse kick, while Carolyn easily handled the other. These "antics" only fuelled the crowd's fury. A hail of missiles assailed the pair and they pressed on. Carolyn was cursing still.

Felix looked around desperately. There was nowhere to hide. Not only was the mob hot on their trail, but people were also barring their housesto deny the pair safety and to save their property from the mob's blind rage. More stones flew at them. Women were ululating and dogs were barking. Storage urns, stalls, chairs and tables, laundry, statues, potted plants: everything was being knocked about. And the crowd was screaming more heatedly than ever, *"Romani, Romani!"*

And then Felix spied it, over in the distance. It was a strange-looking monument, grand but sombre. It was six stories tall and built of blinding-white marble. He couldn't see the bottom half, but its upper one consisted of columns in a square, all surmounted by a pyramidal roof. It wasn't a government building, a temple or palace. What on earth ...?

Felix grinned. This structure was a tomb! And not just any tomb, but ...

"Turn ... right ... next ... corner!" he gasped, wiping sweat from his eyes. His throat felt like leather that has dried and cracked. Carolyn just nodded. She needed all the breath she had.

The corner appeared and they dashed around it. Objects hit the ground in their wake: fruit, stones, sticks, pots, tiles, bricks, and several spears. The crowd was hurling anything at hand. *"Romani, Romani!"* their battle-cry continued. Unwisely, Felix glanced behind. He was shocked to see people flooding the street in a wave. They numbered in the hundreds now and all without exception were charging toward them. *"Romani, Romani!"* A cloud of dust arched over their masses and made it seem that they were part of a tornado. Here and there metal flashed: spears, swords, and knives. The yelling was so loud and persistent that it seemed to be erupting from some beast of prey, the mythological sphinx, perhaps.

They pressed forward. They were panting heavily and on the brink of collapse. Both were soaking and half-dying of thirst.

"Where … to?" Carolyn gasped.

"There!" Felix croaked, steering her left. The tomb lay dead ahead of them and its bottom half was visible. It was built from marble blocks, stacked three storeys high. Stairs were chiselled into these heights. The tomb was thirty metres off. If they could just hang on …

"Can't … run …" Carolyn panted.

"Almost … there!"

Grasping their objective, the crowd pushed harder. More missiles flew. Dates, onions, and oranges assailed him and a stone bounced off his shoulder blade. A tile hit Carolyn square on her neck. She would have lost her balance if Felix hadn't steadied her. Ten metres more....

A guy man appeared beside him, a stick in hand. Felix swung and knocked him flat. Five metres ... four.... Another lout came charging. *"Romani!"* he screamed, his face distorted with hate. He lunged with a dagger. Felix twisted hard and the man bit the dust. And ... there! They were at the steps! Thrusting Carolyn ahead of him, he climbed the first storey then collapsed in a heap.

He closed his eyes. While part of him was thinking they were safe for the moment, another was thinking a dozen hands would strike and spears and swords would cut him to pieces. He was expecting to be dragged in the dust and to hear Carolyn shrieking in pain beside him. He'd feel the blood leave his body and watch dogs skirmish over his limbs....

Nothing. The only sound was of them breathing. He opened his eyes.

The crowd was standing immediately below, three hundred of them, maybe more. Like Felix, they were breathing hard. They were eyeing these "Romans" with murderous lust, watching quietly, and fingering stones. But no one charged. No one. Without exception, they kept their distance.

Some minutes passed. As the two slowly slowly caught their breath, Carolyn threw Felix a questioning look.

"Why don't they strike?" she asked. Her face was red, her hair was dripping and ... she looked more alive than ever before.

"Out of respect for this building. It's lucky I saw it."

"What's makes it so special?"

"This is the tomb of Alexander, the city's founder. In honour of his memory, you can't hurt people seeking refuge here."

"So we're safe so long as we remain on these steps?"

"That's right."

"What happens when we're thirsty? We can't sit here forever. I was such an idiot to drop that figurine!"

Felix said nothing. Instead he climbed the rest of the stairs. They ended at the level that was lined with pillars. Squeezing between two of these, Felix stepped onto a porch-like structure. Spooked by the crowd, Carolyn joined him.

"What a view," he murmured, gazing west. Before him lay a wealth of buildings, a palace, a complex with multiple wings, a theatre, a gymnasium, shops, warehouses, and an endless harbour. It was thick with ships, mostly military vessels, *triremes*, *tetrereis*, and *tessarakonteres*. These last were over six storeys high and could carry close to four thousand sailors. And beyond these vessels was the glorious sea, blue and radiant; an uplifting sight. Most spectacular was a tower on a nearby island. Felix knew it instantly: the lighthouse of Pharos, a wonder of the ancient world.

"I hate to interrupt," Carolyn said, "but this is no time for sight-seeing."

"In actual fact," Felix said, "I'm looking for something."

"Yeah? Like what?"

"There!" Felix cried, pointing left. "Wave your arms!"

Below him and two blocks away was a group of Romans mounted on horses. They were poised before a massive gate, which Felix knew to be the Gate of the Moon. On the gate's far side was the start of a causeway that led across the bay to Pharos Island. This is where the Romans were camped. Their ships were docked beside the causeway and along the island's inner shore. There were also tell-tale tents in the distance, neatly arranged in rows and columns.

"Milites!" Felix screamed, *"Sumus cives Romani! Succurrite nobis!"* He repeated this five times at least.

"They're coming!" Carolyn cried. "Whatever you're yelling, it seems to be working!"

"I told them we're Romans and called for help. Let's return to the stairs."

They left the pillared "balcony" and descended the steps. Many people had left, but a few dozen remained. They were seated in the dust and biding their time. When the two "Romans" reappeared, they smiled and rose to their feet, convinced the pair was about to surrender. As the two approached the end of the steps, the crowd drew closer, their eyes focused on the *"Romani."*

Their lust for violence had them so distracted that they didn't notice the knights' advance. One moment the square before the tomb was empty; the next it was full of charging horses, all bearing Roman knights whose spears were lowered and meant serious business. The clatter of hooves and trumpet blasts caused the lot of them to scatter. One and all they raced down nearby alleys, without any Roman having to strike a blow.

"Quick!" the leader called to Felix. "Before the crowd regroups! Climb aboard!"

Felix and Carolyn darted forward. Strong hands hauled them onto two chargers, and, as soon as they were settled, the beasts sped forward. A cloud of dust defiled the sky. As fast as they'd appeared, the Romans vanished.

A minute later calm returned to the street. A cat stretched out in a pool of sun. The dust slowly settled in place, leaving streaks on people's roofs and awnings. And the resting place of the great Alexander was once again steeped in the quiet of death.

Chapter Sixteen

The sun was hanging low on the horizon. Within an hour it would touch the sea and either die in its waters or set them afire. The day's heat was diminishing and a breeze was blowing in from the west. While the coolness was a welcome change, it meant the world had caught its second wind. The locals were stirring and their thoughts would turn to battle.

Felix crossed the circular room to its eastern window. The Heptastadion was just south of him; it was the causeway that they'd ridden across with their Roman escort. Anchored alongside it was a fleet of Roman *quadriremes*, each with a prow of reinforced bronze. At the causeway's end stood the Roman camp: the legionnaires were getting their dinner ready. They were wise to eat, Felix considered. They had a trying night ahead of them.

Felix smiled as he saw troops scurrying below. They'd treated him and Carolyn well, providing them with food and water and tending their wounds. Felix had hoped that they'd forget the pair, allowing them to melt away when the coast was clear. Unfortunately, Caesar had discovered their presence and wanted to take a look at these strangers. After giving them time to catch their breath, a centurion had finally led them off, even as the legionnaires had wished them luck.

They'd been taken to the lighthouse, where Caesar was quartered. This tower had taken Felix's breath away. It was forty storeys tall and consisted of three levels. The bottom one was square in shape, twelve metres wide and eighty metres tall. It was fitted with dozens of rooms, all beautifully furnished. The second level was octagonal in shape, forty metres high and eight metres wide. Capping it was the final stage, fifteen metres high and circle-shaped. It was four storeys tall and they were standing in the lowest one. The tower was poised on a huge, stone platform and all of it was built from limestone blocks, each weighing a couple of tons. Felix had been in taller buildings, but the height of this one seemed more impressive.

"It seems taller than our buildings," Carolyn said, reading his thoughts. She was with him at the window and admiring the view. Below them was a harbour and … Alexandria. Lights from household fires were burning and the streets were starting to fill with people, especially the area nearest the docks.

"That's our target," he observed. He was pointing to a complex with multiple wings. "The entire building is called the Museion. The library's inside it, right next to the docks."

"It's quite something," Carolyn said, without her usual scorn.

"It is," Felix agreed. "Yet in just a few hours almost all of it will burn. There are a million scrolls inside and most will vanish. All of that learning. It will never be replaced."

"It's strange that information can hang by such a thread."

"That's why we've kept the Repository going. If Angstrom closes it, do you know how much culture we'll lose? Poems, novels, recipes, songs, ideas, dreams, visions of the past. None of this," he said, waving his hand across the city, "none of this will be remembered. It will be as if it had never existed."

Carolyn nodded slowly. For once she actually seemed impressed.

"And what's true of them is true of us, or so my dad always says. If we don't remember the last generation, the next generation will forget us just as quickly."

Even as he finished speaking, he realized that he cared about the Repository's books. His father's guilt still troubled him, but it shouldn't mark the collection's death. If Angstrom tried to shut things down, Felix would fight him tooth and nail.

A noise broke in on them — it was like an ogre snorting. It was followed by a roar-like hissing and Felix thought there was an engine running.

Realizing what it had to be, he stuck his head outside and craned his neck upward. The sky was on fire, the patch above them at least. The dark had advanced and the lighthouse keeper had lit the beacon. It would burn continuously until the following dawn.

"You mentioned your dad," Carolyn said, once Felix had drawn his head back in.

"What about him?" Felix asked, his smile quickly fading.

"I'm sorry he's in trouble. I liked him, until he cloned me, that is."

"To tell you the truth," Felix said uncertainly, "I don't think he cloned you. He might not be behind these attacks."

"I know he's your father, but you shouldn't make excuses."

"I'm not. I really think he might be blameless."

He explained his doubts. If his dad had cloned Carolyn, there were just two places he could have done so. After recovering from the plague, he'd spent his time at home or at the Book Repository. The house was out of the question; Felix and his mother would have caught him red-handed. As for the Repository, there'd been one possible room, but Felix had found nothing suspicious inside it.

"That's something, but it's weak," Carolyn said. "It doesn't explain the pencil, the Zacron suit, or the shuttle's log. And Dr. Lee picked him out …"

"Do you know the professor's wardrobe?"

"In his office? Sure."

"The door is loose and keeps swinging open. When we were with him, I saw inside it. In addition to all sorts of junk, guess what I found?"

"Tell me."

"A pencil stub."

"A pencil stub? That's peculiar."

"And while I didn't see a Zacron suit, I'll bet he owns one. And even if he doesn't, he could have lifted fibres from my father's suit the last time we saw him."

"And the shuttle?" she demanded. "According to its log, it left your house and flew to the Station. Your dad was on it a few hours before."

"True. But while we were heading to the Space Hub to drop my mom off, the professor made a point of calling. He was wishing her good luck, but ..."

"What are you saying?"

"I don't know."

"And even if MacPherson were guilty, what's his motivation? And what about the doctor? He'd have to be lying when he said your dad attacked him. It sounds pretty lame, if you want my opinion."

"I suppose it does," Felix said, shaking his head. "I'm only saying my father's guilt doesn't seem as iron-clad. There's another piece of evidence, but it's probably a long shot. Still, until his guilt is proven, I'm assuming he might be innocent. It's the least I owe him."

"I guess that's true." Carolyn sounded doubtful. Abruptly, she changed the subject. "What are we going to do when we're finished here? I mean, assuming we succeed, how do we get back? I could kill myself for dropping that statue!"

For the next minute they discussed possible solutions. They could return to the stall and try tracking down the portal, but that would mean braving the locals again. Felix, too, could jump to the future, fetch a second portal, and return to the past, never mind the energy this would require. As they debated these choices, an official entered the room. He was of middling height and narrowly built, with fair hair, dark brown eyes, and skin so smooth it resembled a baby's. There was something menacing about him and Felix eyed him closely.

"Caesar will see you," the man said in a nasal tone. "But you must be quick. The general is busy."

Felix knew who he was before he'd finished speaking. As the man left the room and motioned them to follow, he whispered to Carolyn, "That's Marcus Junius Brutus."

"Who?" she asked.

"He fought with Pompey at Pharsalus. Caesar likes him. Too bad he doesn't know the rat will one day kill him."

"Ah," Carolyn said, "and you can't warn him."

"No."

The pair followed Brutus up a flight of marble stairs. One floor up they passed a room like theirs in which a woman and three servants were seated. The lady had jet-black hair, a sculpted nose, and was garbed in Egyptian dress. Again Felix gasped. He only spied her for an instant — Brutus was calling — but realized this was Cleopatra, future queen of Egypt and Caesar's "girlfriend." He couldn't wait to tell his father …

His father. No. That wouldn't work.

"Go in. He's expecting you," Brutus said, when they'd joined him on the next floor. He was pointing to an open door. A servant sat beside it on a stool. There was a storey above them but it held the lighthouse beacon.

They passed the servant and entered the chamber. Brutus closed the door behind them. The space was circular, like the rooms below, and contained a bunk, a desk, and several chairs. There was also a frame holding a set of armour. In addition to the light from the dying sun, three terra cotta lamps cast pale yellow haloes.

"Welcome," a voice hailed them. A figure was at the window and gazing at the scene below. Before Felix could speak, the figure faced them: Julius Caesar.

Felix and Carolyn almost jumped in shock. They'd last seen Caesar three days ago, but in actual fact, twenty-three years had passed; trying ones for Caesar, and the effects were telling. His chestnut hair had whitened and was drastically thinner. His body was lean, but moved less fluidly; his right leg limped, most likely from a battle wound. His skin was leathery, almost like a turtle's, and his eyes, while intensely alive, betrayed weariness and resignation, as if time had tested all his ideas and they'd failed to pass muster. His left fist was clenched. There was something inside it.

His gaze was focused on them. Without speaking he absorbed their presence, their fair complexions, their height, their perfect teeth. His eyes were bright and didn't miss a single detail.

"I know you," he said in a flat, even voice.

"I don't think so," Felix lied.

"We dined together," Caesar insisted. "Crassus was our host. This was when Spartacus was still at large. Your cousin ate with us — I recognize her scar." He pointed to the mark on Carolyn's bare shoulder. "The following day we went to the baths."

"How's that possible, *dux*?" Felix asked, in a jocular tone. "Spartacus was active over twenty years ago. My cousin and I are all of sixteen so …"

"Aceticus was there, the historian. Remember? He was stabbed in two places. I thought he would die, but he climbed to his feet after you worked your magic on him."

"You must be mistaken, *dux*. We know no magic and age like everyone else."

"The pair of you vanished," Caesar said insistently. "Your cousin ducked into the crowd, while you melted like ice on a hot summer day."

"With respect, *dux*. You are describing gods. We're flesh and blood like you."

Before he could finish, Caesar moved with deadly speed. He whipped out a knife and held its point to Felix's throat. Carolyn stepped forward, but checked herself. She couldn't lay a finger on Caesar, not without risking a huge butterfly effect.

"You're right," Caesar spoke with icy calm. "Gods don't need rescuing from angry crowds. You're all too human and will die if I stick you. Unless you care to tell me the truth. Now admit it. We ate with Crassus, Aceticus, and Cicero."

"You've omitted one name," Felix gasped, grasping that he would have to come clean, but hoping to throw the general off-balance. "Gnaius Pompeius Magnus was present, as well."

"How dare you mention him!" Caesar yelled. "No one says his name in my presence!"

"Why? Because your former friend is dead because of you?"

For an instant, Felix thought he'd gone too far. The fire in Caesar's eyes was so out of control that Felix almost felt it scorch his skin. The general's teeth were bared, his nostrils flared, and a growl was mounting at the back of his throat. Carolyn swallowed hard. There was no way she could stop him.

Just as quickly his expression changed. It was like glass shattering from the blow of a brick. "Pompey," he gasped in a strangled voice. He took two steps away from Felix. "Pompey," he repeated, his tone even sadder. His knife slipped from his fingers and fell to the floor. "Pompey," he spoke a third time, looking out the window to conceal his grief.

A roar intruded from outside. It was coming from the city's docks, on the far side of the harbour. Masses were assembling and creating a ruckus. The sun had set. A full moon was peeping over the horizon, casting an orange glow over the city. Ten thousand torches beat the shadows back. To judge by a thousand pinpoints of metal, these were soldiers getting ready for combat. Caesar didn't care.

"You're right," he sighed. "Once upon a time we were the best of friends. He married my daughter and furthered my prospects. I was surrounded by vipers and he kept them at bay. He was frank, generous, and true to his word. Without him, I would never have been consul or been awarded legions to subjugate Gaul. I liked him. No, I loved him. And now he's dead. He was stabbed here in Egypt and I was shown his head. They killed you like a cockroach, my dearest Pompey."

The moon was stroking Caesar's features. Felix was shocked. The general was trembling and tears trickled down his cheeks.

"And he is not alone in death," he continued. "There are many who opposed my rise. They preferred to fight me, to die in battle, rather than calmly accept my rule, and die they did, by the tens of thousands, Romans, citizens, senators, my countrymen. And then there are the Gauls I slaughtered. For the glory of Rome, they were given a choice: yield or die. They too chose war and in numbers past counting they littered the soil. Everywhere I've gone, and I've seen much of the world, death has followed in my wake; sorrow, tears, and destitution. Friends and enemies have tasted death at Caesar's hands. That day I crossed the Rubicon? Jupiter should have struck me with his lightning bolt."

Across the harbour and along the docks, the Egyptians' ranks were swelling. Wagonloads of weapons appeared. There was a clash of metal, the tumult of movement, and the clangour of troops getting ready to fight. And they weren't preparing to war on land alone. Ships were overflowing with sailors, most of whom were wearing armour. The upcoming battle would be no small matter.

"But I'm not to blame," Caesar spoke, as if in a trance. "My honour was always dear to me, but it was not the primary source of these woes. The true cause of this strife has been cold, hard Reason. It is Reason that pushes Rome to expand. It is Reason that insists men shouldn't be different, that their variations should be weeded out, so that all will think and plot the same and love their neighbour as they love themselves. It is Reason that necessitates lies, bribery, arms, and battle. Reason argues borders must be expanded, that the new should crowd out all things old, that men must learn to speak one language, that one culture should guide us, one law should judge us, and one city should rule over all the world. Precise, sharp, unfeeling, and unanswerable, Reason urges humans to ignore memory, tradition, friendship, and laughter, and to advance with our eyes on the future alone, and never to glance at our origins with longing. So Reason dictates. And so I have acted."

There was a cry of triumph as several wagons caught fire. They were piled high with bales of straw and the flames spread a ghostly light across the harbour. Felix trembled. Ten thousand men and more stood armed. The ships were bristling with a freight of spearmen. Far from concealing their numbers, the Egyptians were parading them to frighten their foe.

There was a knock at the door and Brutus appeared. Startled from his reverie, Caesar turned to the doorway.

"The enemy is mustering. They will attack before dawn."

"I'll be down momentarily," Caesar said, moving from the window to the centre of the room. "In the meantime, rouse the troops. And send in Nicias."

Brutus left and was replaced by Caesar's servant. At a nod from Caesar, he approached the wooden frame with the armour and began the process of arming the general. He fastened *pteruges* around his waist, a "skirt" of leather strips. He also took gold-plated greaves from the frame and strapped them firmly to Caesar's shins.

"What am I to make of you?" Caesar asked, his gaze fixed on Felix. His emotions were in check and his face was hard. "I'm owed an explanation. Should I force one from you?"

"Only you can decide that, *dux*," Felix answered. "For my part, I can only warn you. By pressing me to explain, you approach another Rubicon. On one bank lies the world you live in and forge to suit your will. Across its waters is a realm that you can't enter. Even knowledge of its nature is strictly forbidden. If you cross this river and force me to explain, you'll cause more damage than you can possibly imagine. You said you regret having crossed the Rubicon. If so, forget this second stream and allow us to accomplish what we've set out to do."

Caesar would have spoken, but the slave was strapping his breast-plate on. This was a shirt of metal that showed two wrestling lions. Felix had never seen anything so lovely. But it paled in comparison to

Caesar himself. His eyes were closed and Felix used this moment to regard him. Yes. He grasped the source of the man's inner greatness. He was unsparing in his logic when reason was required, yet generous with his humanity when emotion was called for. His eyes suddenly opened and he considered Felix.

"After my first years in Gaul," he said, "I lost faith in Reason and decided to worship at a different altar." He opened his left fist, which he'd been keeping tightly clenched. Inside it were four knucklebones. "Fortuna became my goddess of choice. Instead of treading Reason's path, I have relied on her to guide me as she pleases."

"What does she tell you about us?" Felix asked.

Caesar surprised Felix. He broke into a smile, an expansive show of pity and warmth.

"She says any general can lead an attack. The best generals know when to retreat, as well. I won't press you to explain yourself. And if I can help with something, you need merely ask."

"Thank you, *dux*. You have already been most helpful by withholding your questions. But if you could spare a rowboat, my cousin and I would be most grateful."

"Consider it done," Caesar said, as Nicias tied his *cingulum* in place. "Once we leave this room, we will talk no further. I wish you much success in your mission. And now I have a parting gift."

He held out his hand with the four *astragali*. Felix gasped. He was pleased beyond words with Caesar's offer, but how could he take his tokens of Fortuna?

"If my suspicions are correct," Caesar explained, observing Felix's hesitation, "my course is fixed and Fortuna will not change it. But maybe she can help you out. When you tire of Reason, my mistress will be glad to whisper in your ear."

He smiled again. For a moment the entire room was bright and the room seemed suddenly warmer from the heat of his feeling. Then duty beckoned, his features hardened and he exited the room.

Felix heard his steps echo down the stairwell. Although the general was mere steps away, two millennia already stood between them.

Chapter Seventeen

Felix was holding his body still. He was trying to merge with the dark and to keep his breathing soft and even. Carolyn was doing the same, as were Caesar's soldiers who surrounded them. For the last three hours they'd been standing in formation on the causeway joining Pharos Island to the city. A mist from the sea was stealing round them, condensation was beading on their armour, and their muscles ached from waiting so long, but even a short rest was out of the question. Battle could erupt at any moment and they couldn't afford to be caught off guard.

When the Egyptians had deployed for battle, they'd done so with great fanfare. Then gradually their shouts had died and, like the Romans, they'd stood and waited in silence. For the last two hours they'd been still as death. Their front ranks were visible a short ways off, but these troops weren't daring to breathe or cough. The same was true of the Egyptians at sea. When they struck, they would do so with the stealth of a shark.

Felix glanced at the rowboat moored below them. At Caesar's directive, Brutus had found them the boat. He'd also told them to remain on the causeway until the fighting broke out. If they left before, they'd draw the enemy's fire. One way or the other, the risks were huge.

Felix rubbed his legs to keep the blood circulating. His stomach was half raw with tension and his mouth dry as sand. He wished more than anything that the action would start. Even war would be easier than this infernal waiting. How long had it been? Three hours? Four? It felt more like an eternity.

Carolyn looked his way. Her eyes said it all. She too was impatient and wanted the show to begin. He was just about to whisper something when … they got their wish.

There was a rush of motion. Moments later a dozen fires broke out, half a kilometre ahead of them. In the burst of light that these fires produced, Felix saw that more wagons had been piled with hay and rolled toward their general position. The lead Roman troops weren't expecting this tactic. They raised their shields and locked them together, but the wagons punched a hole in their line.

There was a wild shout from the start of the causeway. As the Romans were shoving the wagons aside and legionnaires were rushing to fill any gaps, their foes sallied forth from the Gate of the Moon and from behind their barricades along the docks. The sound wave formed by their collective shouts practically knocked Felix into the sea. Arrows fell by the hundreds on the Romans, as well as stones from a thousand slings. The resulting sound was horrific and ear-splitting: it was like standing beneath a tin roof in a hailstorm. And besides the racket, the effects were deadly. Felix saw men collapse, one with an arrow sticking out of his throat. He twitched all over; and then was still.

Trumpets sounded. A hail of arrows sailed forth from the Roman line: a third of them had fiery tips and seemed to slice the very night to ribbons before dipping to earth and ripping into the Egyptians. Still, they ran forward by the hundreds and thousands. More trumpets sounded on the Roman side. Before their notes had died, the legionnaires were stirring. The troops' first steps were tentative and clumsy, then their ranks locked tight, their discipline caught fire, and they were muscling forward like one hulking machine.

"This is it!" Carolyn cried. "Let's get moving!" Reaching for a ladder on the causeway's side, she used it to lower herself into the rowboat. When she was seated, Felix followed behind. A deafening sound accompanied his efforts. The front troops on either side had crashed into each other. Shields collided, spears struck home, swords clashed together ten thousand times over. Screams of rage mixed with the howls of men being skewered. The air vibrated like glass about to shatter. *This is the music of death*, Felix thought.

Not that there was time to think. This was their only chance to strike out for the library. It lay half a kilometre from the start of the causeway and was marked by a stretch of docks before it. If they proceeded at a thirty-degree angle, they would have a kilometre of sea to cover. The trick was to avoid being seen by the Egyptians. A Roman, too, could confuse them in the dark and send the odd projectile flying. There was one way to succeed and a hundred ways to fail.

Sitting beside Carolyn, Felix raised the right oar. At a nod from her, he shoved off from the causeway. They were floating between two shifting *triremes* and had to avoid one without hitting the other. By rowing furiously, they quit the shore and entered into the thick of the harbour. A westerly breeze produced a slight swell.

"Head more to port," Carolyn said.

"I always forget which way is port," Felix grunted, straining at his oar.

"Bear left. That's better." Did she say this with a glint of humour?

"The sun's rising," he observed. He was right. A band of sluggish pink and purple was faintly visible beyond the city's eastern limits.

"We have to hurry," Carolyn gasped. "We have to escape this madness while the darkness lasts."

And madness it was. The fighting was at its most brutal now. The exchange of blows was growing more frantic; both sides were straining as hard as they could, and still they were equally balanced, like wrestlers unable to get the best of each other. Men were spilling over the causeway's sides and the din of shouting was so persistent that it sounded like one block of sound, not the product of ten thousand men screaming. One soldier — Roman, Egyptian, who could say — was standing on a length of wall with a spear through his middle. He was doing his best to keep aloft — to fall was to die, he understood clearly. But someone shoved him and he tottered over, to the causeway first, then into the water.

"You're too much to the port, I mean left," Carolyn cried.

"Okay," Felix said, pulling hard on his oar. His biceps were on fire.

"It's not much farther," she said. "Maybe five hundred metres."

No sooner had she spoken than a deep-toned booming assailed their ears. It was rhythmic, continuous, and vibrated in their bones.

"Uh-oh!" Carolyn yelled. "We've got company coming!"

She was pointing left. Through the thin mist hovering above the water's surface and the crack of dawn eating into darkness, a line of shapes was speeding toward them. The Egyptians had finally launched their ships to complement the forces struggling on land. Three ships were larger by far than their brethren — *tessarakonteres*. Each held thousands of troops and would cause the Romans no end of trouble.

"When Caesar sees these boats he'll take precautions," Felix panted. "He'll set fire to his transports and push them afloat, hoping they'll crash into the enemy's vessels."

"What do we care?" Carolyn exclaimed.

"They'll veer off course and set the library ablaze. We have to get inside before the fire catches."

He redoubled his efforts. Despite the breeze and chill in the air, he was pouring sweat. At the same time he was worried that a ship might spy them and chase them down. By swinging right, they could avoid the flotilla, but still a captain might decide to hunt them. If so, they'd be shot at unless they were rammed and crushed to splinters.

"Almost there," Carolyn gasped. She was right. The docks weren't far off and, behind them, stood the library's rear. Before Felix could smile, something whizzed past his ear.

"They're shooting!" he cried. Fifty metres away, a boat was speeding by, its three banks of oars keeping time to a drum. Poised on this *trireme* was a collection of archers. They could see the rowboat and were trying to hit it. *Thwwt, thwwt, thwwt.* Three more arrows went hissing by. One buried itself in the rowboat's side. Drawn by this sport, more archers appeared.

"They have us in their sights!" Felix growled. "Take a deep breath and jump overboard!"

Carolyn was slow. That's why Felix threw his weight to one side and capsized the craft. Even as it flipped, its hull was hit by several arrows. Striking the water, the pair dove beneath the surface. The water was black and hardly reassuring, especially when arrows sliced through its depths — one grazed Felix and tore a hole in his tunic. They swam underwater as far as they could, broke the surface, and swallowed more air before ducking back into the depths. They repeated this process several times, being sure to stick close to each other. Felix fretted that the ship would chase them, but no, it stayed within the flotilla.

"We're out of range," Felix gasped, coming up for air.

"Better yet," Carolyn coughed, "we've reached our goal."

She was right. The docks lay dead ahead of them. Curls of mist whorled about them; buffeted by the swell, their planks were creaking slightly. Best of all, not a soul was in sight.

They swam the remaining fifty metres. Aiming for the side of the dock, they found a ladder and climbed its rungs, quiet but for the water streaming from their tunics. They glanced round nervously, seeing threats everywhere. Their apprehension was groundless. All hell was breaking loose on the causeway, but the docks were clear.

"What now?" Carolyn whispered. She had her arms wrapped around her and was trying not to shiver.

"We break into the library," Felix said. "But that might not be easy."

He moved across the dock, keeping low. His eyes roved everywhere, on the lookout for Egyptians and Carolyn's clone. The roar in the distance set his nerves on edge.

Ahead of them was a three-metre wall. It marked the start of the library's precinct. He stooped and wove his hands together. Carolyn set a foot on his hands and, as he launched her upwards, scrambled up the wall. Then it was Felix's turn. He ran at the wall and dashed halfway up its stone when Carolyn caught him and hauled him to the top. She then jumped into the garden below. Before following, Felix glanced behind.

A dozen fires raged beside the causeway: they were edging through the sea, toward the Egyptian fleet. Felix grimaced. Caesar had already fired his ships. Very soon one of them would crash into the dock and set its wooden planks ablaze. Sparks would enter the library and…. There was no time to waste. He joined Carolyn below.

The garden was a lovely precinct with a fountain, flowerbeds, and busts of ancient thinkers. Felix was reminded of his terrace back home. Following a path, they approached the building. Its walls consisted of limestone blocks, with two-centimetre cracks between each one.

"We can scale the wall," Felix whispered. "The cracks will give us toe-holds."

"I have a better idea," Carolyn replied, pointing farther down. "You see that door? I think it's open. It also looks unguarded."

Before Felix could answer, she sidled in closer. Trailing drops of water, she reached the door and pushed it slowly. She crossed the threshold and vanished from sight. With a pang of worry, Felix rushed forward. Had she run into trouble? Had the guards been alerted?

His fear was uncalled for. She was crouching over a guard who was lying motionless at the foot of some stairs. Felix looked at her questioningly. She shook her head.

"This isn't my doing."

"She's here," Felix said, his blood freezing over.

"I was hoping she wouldn't make it. I guess we're resourceful, my twin and I. I'm just surprised she hasn't set the building on fire."

"It makes sense that she hasn't," Felix said. "All of this will burn soon, yet Aceticus' scroll will survive somehow. If she wants to destroy it, she has to find it first."

"So what's your plan?"

"That's easy. We find it before she does. And we have an advantage. She can't read Greek and her Latin's terrible."

Between them, they carried the guard into the garden, so that he'd be safe when the building caught fire. Returning to the library, Felix closed the door, threw its bolt, and looked around. They were in a marble corridor. On a nearby shelf was a lighted lamp. Farther down there were yet more shelves, each carrying a lamp as well. Every lamp was set in a box of sand to minimize the chance of a fire starting. The second shelf alone was empty: the clone had grabbed its lamp so she could see her way.

Helping himself to a pair of lamps, Felix handed one to Carolyn. He headed down the corridor with care, as if a giant spider were about to jump out. After proceeding five metres, he came upon a doorway. Peering into it, he felt his muscles slacken.

"What is it?" Carolyn hissed. "Can you see the clone?"

Felix didn't answer. He was transfixed. Before him was a spacious room, with marble floors and a panelled ceiling. It was twenty metres long, had a table and chairs, and pillars set at even intervals — their fluting was Greek and the capitals Egyptian. But the walls were the part that interested him. They had floor-to-ceiling shelves that were neatly stacked with scrolls. Spying a line of writing on a column, Felix brought his lamp in close and looked it over. It read (in Greek) TRAGODIA AI.

He swallowed hard. Stretching out his free hand, he took a scroll from a shelf. It carried a tag that read: AGAMEMNON. His fingers trembling, he returned the scroll and took another. ALCMENE was its title. The next read AMYMONE, then ARGO, ATALANTA, ATHAMAS, BASSARAI …

"Felix? What's wrong?" Carolyn asked. "Your face is white and your legs are shaking."

"They're all here," he gasped, barely able to breathe. "Everything's here."

"What are you talking about? What's all here?"

He turned to face her. How could he explain? How could she grasp the value of this treasure?

"I'm holding the lost plays of Aeschylus," he said. "He wrote ninety of them altogether, but only seven survived. Yet here they are. All of Sophocles, too. And then there are the poets who didn't make it, Choerilus, Bion, Eupolis, Lasus, Moschus, Clephon, Phrynichus, and others. Can you guess how much beauty is here? How much learning? Humour? Science? Wisdom?"

He closed his eyes. His job was clear. He had to pile some of these scrolls together and convey them to the future. There he'd study them and add to his knowledge of the ancient world....

"Felix!"

The question: what should he rescue? In that one room alone there were twenty thousand scrolls. Even if he stripped and made a bag of his tunic, he could carry only a hundred pieces. So what should come and what should stay...?

"Felix!"

Should he take the plays of Aeschylus or rescue an author whose works had vanished altogether? Callimachus, for example, existed in fragments, as did Archimedes, Epicurus, Democritus, and Thales. And there were dozens of lost Roman authors....

He felt a smack followed by a red-hot pain. Opening his eyes, he dodged a second slap from Carolyn.

"Why'd you hit me?" he asked, backing out of reach.

"To bring you to your senses. I know these scrolls are precious, really. But you have to focus on the task in hand. If my clone finds that scroll, we won't have any home to return to. Not that I can get home without my statue."

Felix nodded slowly. Fighting his desire to tuck it away, he replaced the scroll he was holding, moved off from the shelf and walked back to the hallway. It ran on for a good fifty metres and had rooms leading off on either side. Each door bore a plaque describing the room's precise contents.

"That's comedy," he said, pointing to a door on his right. "There's more tragedy and, over here, epic and lyric."

They had to turn right at the end of the hallway. It led them past additional rooms — which were filled with more Greek literature — and ended in a corridor that veered right again. After following this third passageway, whose rooms were filled with more scrolls in Greek, they wound up at the door leading into the garden.

"Upstairs," Felix said, pointing to the stairs. He climbed them swiftly two at a time with Carolyn just inches behind. The second floor's layout was like the one below, with a *U*-shaped corridor and rooms on either side. Ducking into the first room — it contained the Greek geographers — he looked outside the window to his left. As he feared, a large, burning object was approaching the shore. Caesar's transport had drifted off course and would collide with the dock in a matter of minutes. It would consume all this learning and …

He tore down the corridor to distract himself from the impending loss. More rooms flew by, medicine, biology, mathematics, astronomy, warfare, ethnography, and philosophy/ethics. Empty-handed, they clambered to the next floor.

Its texts were in Aramaic, Hebrew, and Demotic

(or so the different plaques informed him). And the next floor proved equally unhelpful.

"It's started!" Felix shouted from the front room of the fifth floor. "The docks are burning and sparks are flying everywhere. They're coming in through the windows below!"

"Just keep looking!" Carolyn said.

They searched the floor — it contained Egyptian texts. By the time they'd circled back to the staircase, smoke was rising from the lower levels. Sparks were entering the front room too and Felix saw a pile of scrolls catch fire. He knew they had to plan their escape, but first they had to track the *Historiae* down.

"It must be on the top floor!" Even as he spoke, a blast of heat erupted from the window and stairs. He and Carolyn climbed to the topmost level.

They were getting close: the rooms on this floor contained works in Latin. They roamed the corridors, spying plaque after plaque: oratory, architecture, drama, and poets. Opposite the drama room, in the hallway forming the bottom of the *U*, was a door inlaid with panels showing nine different women. These were the Muses. The door showed no plaque, however, so the pair ignored it. Continuing down the hallway, they saw engineering, politics, legal theory, and … history. Felix ducked into this space.

"You'd better hurry," Carolyn said. "The fire's reached this floor."

Felix didn't answer. As the smoke in the space started to thicken, his eyes roamed a series of shelves. In those with authors whose name began with

A, he saw Acilius, Albinus, Alimentus, Antipater, Appianus, Asellio, Augustus, and reams of *Annales*. There was no Aceticus.

"It's not here!" he shouted.

"That makes sense," Carolyn mused. "This room will burn like all the others. That means, his scroll would perish, too. It's somewhere else."

"But where?"

"What about that door we passed? The one covered with those women?"

"It's worth a try. Although it doesn't look good."

"No, it doesn't."

They left the room and retraced their steps. Both were coughing on account of the smoke and the floor was hot, unbearably so: the marble was conducting the heat from below. Felix was worried. The flames were thickening. There was no returning to the lower floors or entering the front room and climbing out a window. With mounting panic, he ran to the door with the Muses painted on it. Mercifully it wasn't locked.

A welcome sight greeted them on the other side. Before them was a "bridge" of stone connecting the library to the rest of the complex. It was enclosed, six feet high, and lined with marble slabs on either side.

"At least we're safe," Felix said.

"What do you think these are?" Carolyn asked, running her hand over the marble.

"I don't know. Are they decoration, maybe?"

Without answering, she pulled at the edge of one slab. It wheeled open, like a cabinet door.

Behind it were a series of shelves, each one packed with additional scrolls. Above them was a plaque that read: *kai ta loipa*. Felix explained this meant "and the rest" in ancient Greek.

"You don't think…?" Carolyn asked.

Felix was rummaging through these works. Some were in Greek, others in Latin, and none were arranged in alphabetical order. He opened a second door, a third, a fourth and … there it was.

It was a small, ungainly scroll. It was torn a little and its ink was smudged, but the words on its tag were clear as day: HISTORIAE SEXTI PULLII ACETII.

"Is that it?" Carolyn asked.

"That's it."

"It's not much to look at."

"No."

"Well then…."

She never finished her sentence. There was a crash as a vase banged down on her skull. Her eyes widened in shock and she crumpled to the floor. Before Felix could react, something struck him in the face. Dimly he spied a hand reach past him, take the scroll, and pluck it away.

Then a whorl of black sucked him under.

Chapter Eighteen

He was out cold for maybe ten seconds. When he came to, the clone was poised in front of the cabinets. "The scroll," he wondered fitfully. There. She was holding it and looking it over. With her free hand, she was pulling a knife from her tunic. Three steps away, Carolyn was a heap on the floor — the real Carolyn Manes, that is.

Desperate to retrieve the scroll, he planned his attack. Eyeing the clone closely, he spied her hands and was deeply shocked. The skin was dry, veiny and cracked. They didn't look like Carolyn's, but the hands of someone older.

A gasp escaped him. Hearing him, the clone approached and brought her face in closer.

This wasn't Carolyn's twin, but an old woman of sixty. Her brow was wrinkled, her cheeks were withered, and her hair was tangle of white and grey. Only the eyes were the same. They were hazel with a dying fire at their core.

"You look surprised," she said, in a gravelly tone. "I guess I've aged even more than I imagined. It's funny, isn't it? I was sixteen when we last sat together."

"How…?"

"It's the accelerated cloning. The more time passes, the faster I age. At this rate, I'll be eighty by dawn tomorrow. And the day after that my heart will stop beating. Not that it matters. I'll have done my job."

"If you destroy that scroll, you know what will happen. I won't read Aceticus —"

"I know exactly what will happen. I was with you when we returned to an empty world. I heard Sajit Gupta's broadcast, as well as my dad's last message. All of it was heartbreaking."

"So why…?"

"I've been programmed to destroy this scroll. It hurts me, really, the same way it's pained me to hit you, but I have no choice. That's why …"

She raised her knife to the scroll. But before she could slash it, there was a flurry of movement: the real Carolyn rolled forward and knocked her twin off balance. At the same time Felix charged, slammed the clone, and grabbed at the scroll. As he reeled it in, he felt a burning sensation. The clone had slashed his ribs with her knife and blood was flowing from a angry-looking gash. The blood was warm as it travelled down his leg, but the wound seemed superficial, thank goodness.

"Felix!" Carolyn cried. She'd rolled off from the clone and climbed to her feet. Her twin, too, had caught her balance and was crouching low. Her knife was at the ready and she was willing to kill. Despite her age, she was deadlier than ever.

"You're bleeding," she observed. Her tone expressed concern and regret.

"He's bleeding because of you!" Carolyn yelled.

"I can't help it. He's interfering. I'm sorry, Felix, really. You can't guess how much I love you but … hand me that scroll or I'll cut your throat!"

"You monster!" Carolyn cried.

"A monster?" she asked, stepping in close with her blade. "I'm you, Carolyn. If I'm a monster, you are, too."

"You're not me! You're just some test-tube freak!"

"Then explain how I know this!" Here the clone sang in a wavering voice, "O mouse whose nose is oh so pink/shall I tell you mousey what I think/ I think no mom is as lucky as I/ I'll love you mousey till the day I die."

"How did you…?" Carolyn trailed off, astonished.

"I remember mom singing to us. I remember, too, the day she died and how we crawled into our closet and cried and cried."

"That doesn't prove anything," Carolyn said. Her tone was even, but her eyes were twitching. "After all, you want to destroy our world!"

"That's something I can't help," she said, laughing slightly. By now she was two steps from her twin. "And at least I'm not cold, like you. If I could,

I'd act on my feelings for Felix, whereas you ..."

"You're a killer!" Carolyn spat at her twin. They rushed each other an instant later.

It was as though they were in an old-fashioned film that was playing in slow motion. The clone drew her knife back, to strike her twin. To distract her, Felix yelled in a deep, drawn out voice, "Don't! You can have it!" He tossed her the scroll and it sailed through the air with the speed of a stone moving through molasses. As the clone spun to catch it, Carolyn landed a side-kick (it seemed like her foot took an hour to strike its target). Falling sideways, the clone dropped to the floor. With the fire roaring on the far side of the door, she struggled to her feet, Felix leaped forward, and Carolyn jumped high in the air (for what seemed like ten minutes) only to land on her twin with a *crunch*. The trio then separated: Felix stood smiling with the scroll in hand, Carolyn assumed a crouching position, while the clone just lay there with a look of pain. In the silence that followed, time jumped back to normal. There was an ugly choking sound and the clone finally spoke.

"Carolyn," she gasped.

"Stay there or I'll hit you again!"

"Carolyn. Felix," she gurgled. Her voice was weak and her breath was spastic. Felix glimpsed the pool of blood before he spied the knife protruding from her chest.

"Carolyn!" he yelled, running to the clone. He ripped her outer tunic off and pressed it to her wound. At the same time he examined the knife: its blade was buried in her heart. The blood was everywhere. It swamped Felix's hands and was pooling round his knees. Despite her many wrinkles, Felix could see Carolyn's face before him. The light was draining from her lively stare.

"Carolyn," he moaned, "stay with us!"

"Carolyn, come closer," the clone pleaded with her twin. With a look that Felix couldn't decipher, Carolyn kneeled and clutched her clone's hand.

"Listen," the clone whispered, "Listen. I know you. Be true to ... your heart. Otherwise ... regret all your life. I know you ... I know ... and you, we could be ... happy. So sorry ... about ... everything. The snow ... sea ... sun ... so beautiful...."

Using the last of her strength, she joined Carolyn's hand to Felix's. Then her eyes opened immeasurably wide and death streamed in, extinguishing her fires in one fell swoop.

Felix was staring at a water fountain. A stone satyr was spitting water from his mouth and the spray was iridescent in the morning light. A short ways off, men were battling the fire that had consumed the library and ten centuries of human thought. And farther on, a roar persisted as Romans and Egyptians still pounded each other, with neither side willing to concede defeat. They were faced with death on every side, but for the moment Felix's only wish was to sit and watch the play of water.

When Carolyn's clone died, Felix had taken the scroll, returned it to the shelf, and closed the marble panel. With this done, he'd been sure the scroll would survive and so allow him to fight the plague down the road. Before leaving, he'd covered the clone with her tunic, blind to the fact that her blood was staining his clothes. As he'd spied her eyes one final time, so wide and abandoned in the face of death, he'd had to steel himself to keep his knees from buckling.

The real Carolyn had been no help. As soon as she'd spied the knife in her twin, she'd stopped speaking. Her eyes had dulled and her spirit had left her, as if she'd killed herself when she'd driven the knife home. She probably had a concussion as well, from the severe blow that the clone had delivered. Hearing footsteps advance, Felix had steered her through a length of hallways, past rooms containing all sorts of exhibits, clothes, tools, weapons, sculptures, as well as beasts of every stripe and colour, some preserved, others mere skeletons. He'd remembered that, among its other functions, the complex had served as a natural history museum. After wandering blindly for twenty minutes, he and Carolyn had finally stepped outside and reached this courtyard with the satyr fountain.

Despite the ongoing battle, and the library's fire, the courtyard was an oasis of sorts. The Egyptians were too busy to pay them notice and he and Carolyn had been sitting these last few minutes, exchanging stares with the spitting satyr.

But Felix's mind was racing. Part of him was thinking of the scrolls that had burned and was furious that he hadn't saved a single one, a lost play perhaps or philosophical treatise. Another part was dwelling on the fallen clone and how ghastly it had been to watch Carolyn die, or her stand-in at least. But mainly he was wondering how they were going to get home. Between them they had one figurine and it bore a single charge. One of them could jump to the future, retrieve two figurines, then rescue the other. But there was no way he could leave Carolyn there, traumatized as she was and with a bad concussion; but for this very reason he couldn't trust her to return. Despite her normal strength of mind, her present state was fragile.

So how were they to leave? He exchanged stares with the satyr. Its mocking smile seemed to say that they were stuck there forever.

"At least we saved our present," he said. Hearing him, Carolyn stirred.

"I killed her," she whispered. "She's dead because of me."

Felix took her hand, which was dead to the touch. He wanted to remind her that her clone had almost destroyed their world, but any such talk would have been futile. The fact was that she'd killed her clone. It was bad enough to take a life, but to kill a version of oneself! Every cell in the victim was a mirror of one's own and ...

He paused a moment. Every cell a mirror…? Yes, because the DNA was identical. That's what a subject and a clone had in common so …

"I think I have it!" he cried. "I can take us home!"

"We're here," Felix panted. "I'm pretty sure this will work."

They were in the temple of Poseidon, god of the sea. It had a double *peristasis* and oversized *cella*. They were standing in the latter, beside a statue of the god, a bearded figure armed with a trident. How strange to think this statue would one day sit in the Space Hub and contemplate the vastness of deep space. Felix was looking nervously about him. While walking to this temple, they'd drawn people's stares, mainly the men who were wrestling the fire. Suspicious of their blood-stained garb, a few had started chasing them. Felix and Carolyn had beaten them to the temple, but it was just a matter of time before the group arrived.

"I know this statue. It's located in the Space Hub. Like every statue from antiquity, it's been charged by the doctor and its default date is our present. From the Hub, you can contact your dad and he'll convey you to the TPM."

Carolyn shook her head, as if to say this wouldn't work.

"It will work. Think. To prevent strangers from jumping to our future, this portal is based on the clone's DNA. But your DNA's the same so the portal should open."

Fists hammered the *cella* door.

"Go!" Felix said, handling his figurine.

She stretched her hand out. When her fingers were an inch from the sea god's beard, she turned, looked at Felix, and gave him a kiss. A second later a yellow light erupted and she was gone. Six men burst into the room just then and Felix bore down on the figurine.

The Egyptians saw a young man smile as time hurled his atoms into the embrace of eternity.

Chapter Nineteen

"Let's begin," the general spoke. "This shouldn't take long."

He exchanged looks with the group about him. They were standing in the chamber with the TPM. Four people stood about him in a ring, Professor MacPherson, Dr. Lee, Carolyn, and Felix. The professor looked his cheerful self, but Dr. Lee seemed more morose than normal. His posture was that of a broken man.

Two days had passed since their return to the present, and the pair had used that time to recover from their trauma. Although she'd slept a lot and been treated for shock, Carolyn wasn't her old self yet. Her eyes were ringed and she had a haunted look. She was talking again, but had little to say, about her adventures or anything else. While he hated to admit as much, Felix felt that Mem-rase might help her. If the procedure allowed her to feel at ease, it might not be a bad idea.

He himself had barely rested. He'd had numerous errands to run, ones he didn't dare postpone. He'd also wanted to check on his dad, who was still sitting among his books without the desire to crack them open. While his fatigue was catching up with him, Felix was glad to keep himself busy. The memory of those burning scrolls would have driven him crazy.

Happily, he possessed a relic from the past. As General Manes brought their meeting to order, Felix clutched four knucklebones. It thrilled him to think they'd last been touched by Caesar. They also gave him the courage to cross another "Rubicon."

"I want to commend my daughter and Felix. It's because of them that, again, we've been saved from the plague. I know I gave you a hard time, Felix, and hope you'll accept my deepest apologies. As for you Carolyn, I can't say how proud I am. You've met my expectations and left them in the dust. It's a pity we can't talk about the TPM, if only to tell the world how much they owe you. Still, for what it's worth, you have our warmest thanks."

Here the general started to clap. Dr. Lee and the professor quickly joined in. Addressing Bernard, the Space Station's system, the general asked for servings of champagne. Instantly five glasses appeared in an alcove.

"To Felix and Carolyn," the general said, holding up his flute.

"To Felix and Carolyn," the professor agreed.

"To Felix and Carolyn," Dr. Lee whispered.

"To unfinished business," Felix added, before sipping his drink. It was delicious and the bubbles tickled his nose. He took a second sip, to fortify his courage.

As he expected, the men lowered their drinks and eyed him warily. Carolyn, too, studied him with interest. She suspected his comment referred back to their chat in the Pharos lighthouse — twenty-two hundred years ago!

"We're not safe," Felix said. "Not while the culprits are free."

"If you're referring to your father," the general said, setting down his glass. "We've established his guilt beyond the shadow of a doubt."

"Are you sure?" Felix asked. "Because if you've nabbed the wrong man, the real criminal's at large and can strike whenever he pleases. And next time around he might succeed."

"Look," the general said, his tone cool and abrupt, "we've covered this already. I'm truly grateful for everything you've done, but I'd rather not rehash the issue. You have to accept your father's guilt...."

Carolyn touched him, her way of urging him to let Felix speak. He turned and glared at her. When she refused to relent, he faced Felix again.

"I'll give you five minutes."

"Thank you. I'd like to show you something in OR3. And Bernard," he called to the station's system, "can you link me up with Mentor, my domestic unit?"

"Processing," Bernard replied.

"My father's arrest started with a pencil," Felix spoke, as he led the way to OR3. "It was one of the factors that led you, general, to show my dad's picture to Dr. Lee. There was also that fibre from a Zacron suit. Dr. Lee confirmed my dad was his attacker and … you know the rest."

"You're forgetting the shuttle," the general said tersely. "The one belonging to your mother's firm. Its log shows clearly that —"

"Its log was tampered with," Felix said evenly. "Yesterday I went to CosmoConn. The CEO, my mother's friend, examined the shuttle's piloting software and found a rogue signal embedded in its hard drive. It infiltrated the shuttle's system while my family and I were being taken to the Space Hub. With it in place, the intruder could ghost-pilot the craft."

"Who's this intruder?" the general demanded.

"And why did I ID your father?" the doctor asked. His eyes were wild and his voice was high.

"I'll get to that later," Felix said. By now they'd reached OR3. It was a tight fit, but they squeezed themselves in. The general looked skeptical, but not as scornful as before. The doctor was nervous, while the professor was his unflappable self. Carolyn stood directly behind Felix, as if watching his back.

"This is cozy," the professor joked.

"It's more than that," Felix said. "Do you see that structure?" He was pointing to the operating bed that, once upon a time, Aceticus had lain on. More than ever, its box-like qualities made it seem like a coffin.

"What are we looking at?" the general asked.

"As a matter of fact," Felix said, "you're looking at a cloning tank." Stepping forward, he reached under a retractable arm. Inside the joint was a hidden switch, which, when pressed, caused the padding on the bed to open. Its interior revealed a hollow space replete with ducts and a tangle of tubes. It also contained a set of cortical implants.

"The ducts allowed for the passage of fluids," Felix explained. "While those tubes admitted nutrients and bio-pharm. And notice the implants. They uploaded these files while the clone was taking shape." He took a blue sphere from a nearby shelf. It was labelled CM I and was part of a series of six. Inserting this into a nearby port, he ordered Bernard to play the contents. A nearby screen revealed a stream of images.

"Cathy!" the general gasped.

"Mom!" Carolyn murmured.

A woman resembling Carolyn filled the screen. She was laughing and shuffling holographic bears — a toy Felix had played with as a baby. Leaning in, she kissed the recording lens — the lens, of course, was Carolyn herself. These images were her memories, which had been digitalized and transferred to the sphere's flash drive.

"The clone was created here," Felix said, "and this is where Carolyn's memories were stolen. Obviously my father had no hand in this business."

The group was silent. Without awaiting their comments, Felix returned to the TPM. The general was frowning and massaging his neck — a sign he was digesting the implications — the doctor looked as white as a ghost and the professor's hands were buried in his pockets. He still looked cheerful, but a touch distracted.

"So you're saying ..." the general said once they'd gathered by the TPM.

"I'm saying your daughter was cloned by Dr. Lee."

"Impossible!" the general cried. "No one is more loyal than Chen!" His eyes flew to the doctor who was staring at the floor. "Chen! Speak up! Look, maybe I was wrong about your father, Felix, but Chen had no reason ..."

"He had every reason," Felix said. "Bernard!" he called out. "Is Mentor online?"

"Affirmative."

"I am here, Felix," a familiar voice broke in. Hearing Mentor, Felix almost smiled.

"Two days ago," Felix told the general, "I gave Mentor a sample from the clone's bloodied tunic. I asked him to determine the fourth date programmed into the tracer."

"We performed tests," the general said. "They were inconclusive —"

"So the doctor maintained," Felix broke in. "But Mentor came up with a different result. Tell us, Mentor."

"The date in the tracer," Mentor said, "is June 6, 2213, 5:34 a.m."

The general gazed at Felix. "So?" he asked. "What does that prove?"

"Shall I tell him doctor?" Felix said. "Or would you like to explain?"

Dr. Lee groaned. He could barely stand. With the utmost effort he tried to speak, but the only sound produced was a meaningless gurgle. Finally, a single word emerged: "Charlie."

"What he means to say," Felix explained, "is that the plague killed his son on June 7, 2213. The clone was programmed to jump to June 6 so that she could hand Charlie the *lupus ridens* and keep him alive. In exchange, the doctor would co-operate."

"Co-operate?" the general asked. "With whom?"

"Come now, Isaiah," Professor MacPherson broke in. "You're usually not so slow. He's talking about me. I persuaded Chen to join my little plot. At my suggestion, he cloned your daughter, programmed the tracer, ran the TPM, and activated portals in the ancient world. He also caused those mini blackouts and helped me with that signal, the one that enabled us to frame poor Eric. This was after I'd devised my plan to send someone back to assassinate Aceticus."

The professor had backed away from the group and was standing just outside the TPM's sphere. Despite his confession, he was as calm as ever. He was smiling kindly, his tone was soft, and his eyes gleamed with their usual good humour. To judge by his appearance, he looked every inch the scholar, and nothing like the monster that he was.

"Ewan," the general said, shaking his head. "I don't understand. How could you?"

"How could I?" the professor asked, not just smiling, but grinning now. "Surely you mean, how could I not? After all, someone had to act. The only candidates were Felix and his father, but they were too 'decent' to get their hands dirty. That left me. There was no one else. And given my years, I had to act soon before I lost my strength of purpose."

"What are you talking about?" the general asked.

"You don't see it?" the professor cried. "No, of course you don't. We're finished as a species, Isaiah. Our passion is spent. The pride, the despair, the hilarity, the rage: these feelings made us what we are, allowed us to triumph over impossible odds, to evolve from the apes into poets and thinkers, yet we've practically rendered them non-existent. The same is true of our most hallowed memories. We owe a huge debt to the ghosts before us, yet we refuse to pay them the slightest attention, as if this," he motioned to the machines in the room, "all of this was the product of our genius alone. War has vanished, yes, and there's no poverty, violence, crime, or sickness. When we awake each morning, we face comfortable prospects and know the day will pass without conflict. But what have we *really* achieved? Sure, we live in comfort, but at the cost of everything that makes us human. With ERR and Mem-rase, we've tossed our very souls aside and turned ourselves into lifeless machines. We don't weep or laugh or grieve or rage? Then we are dead men walking and nothing more. Easy there, Isaiah," he suddenly barked.

General Manes was closing in on the professor. Nonplussed, MacPherson had reached into his jacket and pulled out an old Colt .45. He was pointing it at the general who retreated a step.

"I may seem like a brute," he continued, "but my intentions were lofty. My goal was to reclaim our majesty of old and snap us out of the trance we're in. If the plague were raging in our midst again, we'd have experienced a wide range of emotions, sorrow, rage, and terror, to be sure, but determination and pride, as well, and sacrifice, love, generosity, and triumph. We would have been alive once more! Alive, inspiring, appreciative, and noble! I love humankind too much to watch it toss its higher functions aside. That's why I was ready to sacrifice millions; by doing so I would have resurrected billions. You may think me a madman but I'm a saint in fact."

"Would a saint kill every human on the globe?" Felix asked. "If the plague had returned, we would all be finished."

"I didn't know," MacPherson replied with a shrug, "but even so, I was doing us a huge favour. We are better off dead than living like robots. I regret nothing, nothing, do you understand?"

"But I do," the doctor broke in. "If I'd known the plague would prove so destructive, I'd never have agreed to help the professor. And my decision to bring Charlie back at the cost of others, this was utterly shameful. I was wrong and …"

"You weren't wrong, Chen," the professor said, with a frosty smile. "You were weak and sentimental. And you, Felix, well, I'm disappointed. Besides me, you're the last true human alive. You know exactly what treasures we've lost, and here you are supporting these ERR freaks. I expected better from you. But there's hope yet. I can kill Aceticus myself once and for all. Get back!" he yelled in warning.

General Manes had stepped forward again, along with Felix and Carolyn. The hammer on the gun was cocked and the professor was waving it desperately. Felix was thinking that he should rush MacPherson, even at the cost of a bullet to the chest; after all, he'd die if the old man escaped and managed to get the plague back on track. Even so, his muscles were slow to respond.

"Alea iacta est," the professor said with a death-like grin. He then touched the sphere's see-through door. The gases inside were swirling madly, as if a fateful journey was about to transpire. In a moment the professor would be crossing the threshold. Felix was desperate to attack, but his legs wouldn't let him.

It didn't matter.

"Chen! Let go!" the professor cried. "I'll shoot if I have to...."

The doctor had grabbed his one-time partner and the pair was struggling on the sphere's threshold. Its door was now gaping open and wisps of gas were streaming into the chamber. They curled around the wrestling duo and tugged at their limbs, as if teasing them to give eternity a go. The doctor's hands were on the professor's right wrist, trying to shake the gun free of his grip. The professor was clawing at the doctor's face and screaming and cursing in Greek and Latin. His glasses fell and clattered to the floor. Felix moved forward, but his response was slow, as if an unseen force were holding him back. The doctor forced the professor's hand lower. MacPherson grappled for the doctor's throat. Their bodies swayed violently and spun once, twice, in circles, as if glued to each other and desperate to break free. Felix was five feet off, four, three …

An explosion sounded. It was muffled slightly, but echoed around the chamber and took forever to fade away. Even as Felix came to a stop, the general opened his mouth in fear, and Carolyn swiftly dropped to the floor, the doctor calmly straightened himself, the pistol clenched in his right hand.

For his part the professor looked surprised — no — shocked. Glancing at his stomach, he almost laughed at the sight of a small black hole and a telltale ochre stain on his shirt. The red was spreading swiftly, no, voraciously. Barely able to remain on his feet, MacPherson declared in a shaky voice, *"Fortuna iudicavit,"* meaning: "Fortune has passed judgment."

Before Felix or anyone else could stop him, and before the station's Health Drones could spring into action, MacPherson gathered the last of his strength and collapsed inside the transparent sphere. Like vultures feeding on a weakened victim, the gases churned about him until … he was gone.

"Where…?" Carolyn started to ask.

"In a place where he'll die of that wound," her father answered. "Nothing can save him."

Felix might have added something but his eyes were on the doctor. The pistol still in hand, Dr. Lee was frowning, as if studying a phantom only he could see. While his expression marked his total defeat, his posture was straight and implied strength of purpose.

"Chen," the general called out. "The drama's finished. Please lower the gun."

The doctor turned and looked them in the eye. His face was hollow, as if he'd been a dead man all this while. He smiled and the effect was even more ghastly. And instead of lowering the gun, he had it aimed at his heart.

"What a strange thing passion is," he reflected. "In your case, Felix, it led you to save a world; in mine, it led me to seek its destruction. And all because I loved my boy. I missed him so much that I never considered how he'd react to my actions. He was kind and honest, Charlie was. He'd have been shocked to discover that I had killed to bring him back."

"Chen. Lower the gun," the general pleaded. "We can help you. Mem-rase can ease the pain."

"But I don't want it eased, Isaiah. True, I'd rather not remember my loss, but I can't possibly forget it, either, not without killing Charlie again. And so ... I will take my leave in Roman fashion. Believe me when I tell you that I am so, so sorry for pain I've caused. Farewell ..."

"No!" the general screamed.

"Wait!" Carolyn and Felix pleaded.

"Charlie, I'm coming," Dr. Lee announced.

A shot rang out. Again it travelled round the chamber. By the time its echo had died away, Dr. Chen Lee, loving father of Charlie, had entered a stream of time that coursed on forever.

Chapter Twenty

"**I**'ve entered another algorithm contest. The judges will decide the winner next week, but I know I'm a shoo-in. Carolyn didn't compete this time. I guess she learned her lesson and knows she'll never defeat me."

Felix sighed. Life was back to normal and he was travelling from Toronto to Rome in search of more books. As luck would have it, Stephen Gowan had spied him and installed himself in a nearby seat. The trip was scheduled to last twenty-one minutes. Felix wondered how he'd survive this ordeal.

It had been two weeks since the showdown in the TPM. Besides taking time to heal, Felix had composed a long report and provided evidence against Professor MacPherson. Together with the general and other staff members, he'd attended a funeral for Dr. Lee. Yes, the man had plotted against the world; but he'd also wound up stopping the professor.

Having spent a week tidying the drama's loose ends, he'd boarded a shuttle with General Manes and watched the station recede into the distance. In the wake of the near temporal disasters, it had been decided to shut the facility down. While the TPM had stopped the plague last year, events had shown it was incredibly dangerous. The risks outweighed the benefits and Time was something that shouldn't be toyed with. Apart from a couple of service drones, the Station would be off-limits to all personnel. "That's fine by me," General Manes had joked. "I can at last study history without having to worry you'll change its course." Before parting with Felix, he'd promised to speak before a global council and ensure the Repository would never be closed. "This is a debt of honour," he'd promised. "To you and all the people of the past."

"And speaking of Carolyn, what's with her?" Stephen said, oblivious to Felix's lack of interest. "I saw her at the awards ceremony and she hasn't been in touch since then. She's ignored all my messages and pretty much vanished. What is it with girls? She meets my parents, shares the stage with me, I discuss my techniques and future plans, and she hasn't the decency to stay in touch? Talk about ingratitude!"

Felix sighed again. Carolyn wasn't well. When Dr. Lee had put a bullet through his heart, his suicide had pushed her over the edge. Fragile from her battle with the clone, she'd closed her eyes and collapsed to the floor. As things stood, she was undergoing psychiatric testing. Over the last two weeks, he'd sent her messages daily, but hadn't received any answer back. Who could blame her? As she saw it, Felix was connected with death. The plague, gladiators, Clavius, the wars, Dr. Lee, the professor, the library, the clone: the list rolled on and on. If she was going to put her trauma aside, perhaps she should never see him again, or be reminded in any way of their times together.

But the news wasn't all bad. Once the professor had been proven guilty, General Manes had been in touch with Mr. Taylor. After apologizing for his error of judgment, he'd restored Mr. Taylor to his former self. While he was still raw from his ordeal, Felix's dad was on the mend and expected to recover. Already he was shelving books and busy reading, to the accompaniment of his beloved Bach. Felix and he were still shy around each other, but their relationship would soon be on good footing again. By the time Mrs. Taylor returned, their household would most likely be back to normal.

"Come to think of it," Stephen said, "I haven't seen much of you, either. You look thin and hollowed out. I guess you've been reading all this while, hey? You've been losing sleep over those tales of Caesar who's famous because he invented a salad?

Felix smiled thinly. The sooner he got used to this ribbing, the better. The crisis was over and the world was back to normal. People didn't know how close they'd come to tasting death again. And if they did know, they would quickly forget, by shrugging the business off or undergoing Mem-rase.

But he no longer cared. People were set in their ways and he couldn't change them, not against their will. On the other hand, they couldn't change him, either. Just because they were indifferent to the past didn't mean his interests were without value. He'd known this all along, but now, after Rome, Alexandria, Clavius, and Caesar, he was strong enough to ignore oafs like Stephen Gowan. His course was clear. He would follow it boldly. And if myopic idiots kept interfering ...

"No seriously, why would anyone waste his life reading garbage when he could devise new computer programs? Doesn't it bother you?" Stephen groused. "I mean, really. Here I am, working on important stuff, while you spend your days reading stories to yourself. It's affecting your health. You know what I think?"

"I know exactly what you think," Felix said. "And for someone who's supposedly so smart, you have no idea what you're talking about. So if you don't mind ..."

He disengaged the speaker connecting their pods. Insulted, Stephen kept jabbering away, like a machine playing out its pre-programmed role. Smiling to himself, Felix looked out the window and was dazzled by the sight of clouds passing in a stream.

It was a simple truth, he mused, even if it lacked all logic. The sun would rise tomorrow because it had risen yesterday.

Felix eyed the sky with worry. Clouds were gathering and it was two minutes past three. According to the local reports, rain was scheduled for 3:09 p.m. and would last twelve minutes before it headed south. He had to find some shelter over the next seven minutes.

He was walking through the heart of Rome. He was coming from a nano-bot plant that had been built on a library fifty years back. While the library's contents had long eroded, a large trunk full of books had survived. Opening its lid, Felix had found treasures inside: detective novels, children's books (among them was something called *Harry Potter*), a manual on car repairs, two travelogues, three cookbooks and the *Elvis Repertoire* (whatever that meant). After arranging to have the trunk sent to Toronto, he'd left the place with the cookbooks in hand, much to the amusement of the factory boss.

There was a distant roll of thunder. Understanding he had six minutes to find shelter, Felix glanced ahead. Fenced off from the modern part of town, with its vast commercial centre and so-called floating towers (eight mega-structures built on transparent piles), the ancient Forum seemed to call him over. With a shrug, Felix sprinted forward.

He ran along a road that followed the old Claudian aqueduct. To his right was the Coliseum, and, perched before it, the Arch of Constantine. For a moment he thought of veering off and waiting beneath its pitted stone hollows, but a thought had occurred to him and he knew his destination. It was a structure that, despite its age, would keep him dry.

A small fence confronted him. He leaped and cleared it. The rumbles grew louder and a breeze was blowing in from the west. It smelled of rain.

Ahead of him were trees — poplars planted in a row. He had to twist to manoeuvre past them, but, once they were behind, the ruins lay before him. He smiled as they greeted him like a long-lost friend, the Domus Flaviana, the Stadium Palatinum, the Templum Jovis Victoris, and the Curia Julia.

A raindrop struck. Then another and another. He wanted to run, but the ground was uneven and set with broken lengths of marble, remnants of an ancient past which modern Rome would come to resemble, considering Time never stopped exacting its dues. The rain was really falling. The sound of it hitting the poplars was thrilling and the earth seemed to come alive at its touch. The stones were indifferent. Over the last eighteen centuries they'd been toppled, kicked, hammered, battered, ignored, peed-on, and generally abused, so a summer rain was nothing.

At last he reached the curia. Approaching its doors, he stroked their weathered surface. Much to his surprise, they opened at his touch, creaking eerily on their hinges. While dim, the interior was lit: the building had windows set into its walls and these allowed the afternoon light to enter. Felix advanced to the centre of the room. He glanced up at the vaulted ceiling, at the bits of broken statuary and patterned floor. Finally his gaze alighted on a bust in an alcove. Being careful not to slip on the marble, he made his way over.

It was a bust of Julius Caesar — he had commissioned this building. The general's eyes considered him closely, with suspicion at first then a certain warmth. *So you made it*, they seemed to say.

"I made it," Felix said aloud.

The weight of his struggles suddenly struck home: Aceticus's wound, his brush with ERR, Clavius dying in front of his eyes, the angry Egyptians, the battle at the harbour, the library's destruction, the clone's final gasps, the professor's fall, the doctor's death. A wave of exhaustion almost bowled him over and he felt empty, saddened and … alone. That was the worst part, his isolation. If there were someone to talk to, someone to hold….

Not just someone.

You should call her, Caesar seemed to address him.

"I can't," Felix spoke aloud. "She's fragile and I'm no good for her."

Call her, Caesar insisted. *I saw you together*.

"I shouldn't. I can't."

See what Fortuna says.

Felix stared hard at the bust. After a minute, he put his hand in a pocket and pulled out four *astragali* — the knucklebones that he'd received from Caesar. Rolling them in his hands, he tossed them on the floor. They were light and porous, but there was a faint echo as they clattered off the marble. Felix bent and looked them over. The sides confronting him were different, all of them. Was that a good sign or …?

That's a Venus, Caesar seemed to address him again. *The best possible throw! The love goddess approves and that can only mean one thing!*

Felix stood. He felt dizzy and cold and hot and … hopeful. Standing close to the bust, he stroked its marble cheek, then turned away and approached the exit. The rain was spitting but, over in the west, the clouds were getting thinner. Being sure to close the doors behind him, he rushed across the ruins and replenished green.

He had another Rubicon to cross. But with Fortuna's blessings, he wouldn't take no for an answer.

Glossary

Ab urbe condita	From the founding of the city (i.e., Rome in 753 BCE)
Alea iacta est	The die is cast
Apodyteria	A changing room
Arar	The river Saone
Balineum Fausti	The Faustine Baths
Caldarium	A room containing a hot pool (in a public bath)
Cella	The innermost shrine of an ancient classical temple
Cubit	A unit of length (roughly 45 centimetres)
Cucina	Kitchen
Domine	Lord, master (a term of respect)

Dux	Leader, general
Fili mi	My son
Hortus	Garden
Hostis	Enemy
Laconicum	The hottest place in a Roman bath
Lectus	Couch
Magister	Teacher, master (a term of respect)
Mehercule	By Hercules (interjection)
Munus	Game, gladiatorial exhibition
Palaestra	Exercise grounds in a Roman bath
Patricii	The patricians or Roman noble families
Pax tibi	Peace to you (singular)
Pax vobiscum	Peace to you (plural)
Peristalsis	A colonnade around a temple
Peristylium	A courtyard within a Roman house
Porticus	A colonnade serving as an entrance to a building or temple
Puer	Boy (term of affection)
Rhenus	The river Rhine
Rhodanus	The river Rhone
Sequana	The river Seine
Tamesis	The river Thames
Thermae	Baths
Vicus	A street
Vigiles	The public guard
Vale pater	Hello father

Acknowledgements

I would like to thank Michael Carroll for his willingness to run with another Felix Taylor adventure. I would also like to thank Shannon Whibbs for her immensely helpful corrections and editorial suggestions. The story is much stronger as a result.

Other Dundurn Titles for Young People by Nicholas Maes

Laughing Wolf
A Felix Taylor Adventure (Book 1)
978-1554883851
$12.99

It is the year 2213. Fifteen-year-old Felix Taylor is the last person on Earth who can speak and read Latin. In a world where technology has defeated war, crime, poverty, and famine, and time travel exists as a distinct possibility, Felix's language skills and knowledge seem out of place and irrelevant. But are they? A mysterious plague has broken out. Scientists can't stop its advance, and humanity is suddenly poised on the brink of eradication. The only possible cure is *lupus ridens*, or Laughing Wolf, a flower once common in ancient Rome but extinct for more than two thousand years. Felix must project back to Roman times circa 71 B.C. and retrieve the flower. But can he navigate through the dangers and challenges of the world of Spartacus, Pompey, and Cicero? And will he find the Laughing Wolf in time to save his family and everyone else from the Plague of Plagues?

Transmigration
978-1459702318
$12.99

Simon Carpenter is a normal sixteen-year-old living in Vancouver. Or is he normal? Any type of music drives him crazy. When walking by a homeless person, he can see the world through the drunken man's eyes. And when visiting a pet shop he hears a rabbit speaking to him. To solve these mysteries, he takes the rabbit home, only to discover that a foreign "presence" lives inside it. To make matters worse, this "presence" belongs to an army of souls that has plans to supplant the human race. Who are these creatures? How do they plan to accomplish their goal? How is Simon connected to them? And how can he stop them? These are questions he must answer … quickly. Nothing is what it seems to be and failure will lead to worldwide disaster.

Crescent Star
978-1554887972
$12.99

Avi Greenbaum is Jewish and lives in West Jerusalem. Moussa Shakir is Palestinian and lives in East Jerusalem. Both are fifteen years old, live without their fathers, adore their older brothers, and belong to the same soccer club. Avi commemorates the Holocaust and celebrates Israeli independence, while Moussa mourns on Nakba Day, marking the expulsion of Palestinians from their homes and land in 1948. Their lives are parallel lines: they have everything in common and nothing at all. Each is oblivious to the other's existence. As Avi and Moussa go about their daily routines in the spring of 2006, they face reminders of the conflict that has dogged the region for the past three generations — the security wall, suicide bombings, police operations, and the looming shadow of war. While navigating this legacy of suspicion and violence, they must decide what their own roles in the stalemate will be.

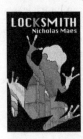

Locksmith
978-1550027914
$11.99

Twelve-year-old Lewis Castorman is a master locksmith: there is no lock on earth that he is unable to open. He is therefore flattered when world-renowned chemist Ernst K. Grumpel invites him to his office in New York City and offers him a lock-picking assignment. His confidence quickly turns to dismay, however, when he learns this job will take him to Yellow Swamp in northern Alberta. He is also horrified to discover that Grumpel is utterly ruthless and, through his chemical inventions, can alter the rules of nature at his will. How is Grumpel able to create such miraculous transformations? What secrets has he locked away? Despite the strange discoveries Lewis will make at every turn in his adventures, nothing will prepare him for the final encounter that awaits him in Yellow Swamp.

 **DUNDURN**